CW00400560

The Beach Hut
by
JENNIE ALEXANDER

Chapter One

Ella hid behind a tree - just in time. She peered around it, looking through the woods towards the church, and waited. The photographer was in position, ready to capture the moment, as Jon and Danielle stepped out into the world as Mr and Mrs Peters. Careful not to make a sound Ella moved slightly for a better view, her shaking hand against the tree trunk to steady herself. And here they came, arm in arm, the happy couple. They looked at each other and laughed. The photographer called for their attention and they obeyed immediately, eager to record their happiness for all to see. The young woman was a typical beautiful bride and the groom - a much older man.

Ella didn't dare move now as the rest of the wedding party emerged from the church. They were ushered onto a pretty green with a backdrop of weeping willow trees for the group photographs. All brides are supposed to look beautiful on their wedding day, Ella thought, and as hard as she tried she couldn't find any fault with the appearance of this one. Ella stared at her as she posed for the camera, her three bridesmaids fussing with her dress and veil. "Yes, you look perfect," whispered Ella. "And maybe you are perfect. Apart from the fact that you stole my husband."

Ella watched for a while longer and then thought she should go, taking a few careful steps backwards, wanting to leave but unable to pull herself away. She was aware that she would pay for every second and that every detail would be painfully replayed for a long time to come. But this was an irresistible quick fix to satisfy her long-held curiosity, like scratching a rash, the pay-off being long term scarring.

Suddenly a voice called out. "Ella!"

Ella froze. Her heart thumped so hard she could actually hear it. Only her eyes moved as she scanned the crowd for the person who had seen her.

"Don't run off like that. Stay where Mummy can see you."

Thank god. Another Ella, in the form of a three year old fairy princess complete with tiara and wings who was now hiding shamefully behind her mother's legs. Grown up Ella put her hand to her chest. She could feel her heart pounding despite several layers of warm clothes.

It was mid autumn and by rights today should have been freezing cold but the new Mrs Peters even had Mother Nature on her side. A cloudless blue sky allowed the sun to squeeze out its last rays of warmth before winter set in, casting long artistic shadows and giving everything a magical glow.

Ella felt a little light-headed. She hadn't been able to face food today. She'd been to the supermarket that morning to keep herself busy and despite a trolley full of her favourite things, nothing could tempt her. And now, the worst thing would be for the groom's first wife to be found having fainted while lurking in the bushes. The thought prompted Ella into action; she turned and quickly returned to her car.

It was dark now and cold. Ella lifted the curtain aside to see a few spots of icy rain hitting the window. She let the curtain fall back into place and returned to the warmth of the room. It won't matter now anyway, she thought. It could rain or hail or even snow and it won't matter because the wedding party will be in full swing and nobody will care what's going on outside. She smiled feebly and snorted a little laugh. She'd had a few glasses of wine and everything was beginning to blur and fade to a welcome fuzziness.

Ella placed another log on the fire, prodded it in place with the poker and tried to make herself cosy under a soft tartan blanket. "At least I got to keep the house. And the decent car. And the beach hut was mine anyway. She can keep the bastard. That's a fair deal." Ella closed her eyes knowing full well she would trade them all to have him back again.

But, she had done it, just as she had planned. Jon was now married to someone else and she had seen it with her own eyes. That was it – all over. And now it was time to move on. Ella lifted her glass from the side table and held it up as a toast to herself but her voice was quiet and shaky. "Here's to me, and new beginnings."

Ella drifted off to sleep where dreams took her climbing up the giant, never ending tiers of a wedding cake. Jon was standing at the top and she was clambering to reach him. Hundreds of three-year-old hideous pink fairy princesses skipped around the cake chanting the wedding march in screechy voices. And the stick-thin skinny body of a ten-foot high bride was bending and bowing as she was buffeted by the wind. Dried leaves and bits of twig caught in her hair and veil until suddenly she snapped clean in half.

Ella awoke in the early hours, cold and headachy. The fire had gone out and it was still dark outside. She unfolded her long legs and slowly stretched her stiff limbs wishing she hadn't fallen asleep on the sofa. She wasn't ready to face tomorrow and certainly didn't want to go over the events of today - she just wanted to sleep. With pins and needles in her left foot and a painful numbing sensation travelling up her leg, she hobbled upstairs and crawled into bed without undressing. But her mind was awake and she couldn't stop her thoughts. When she awoke, she could feel the damp pillow under her cheek from where she'd finally cried herself to sleep.

It was into the afternoon when Ella eventually climbed out of bed. She never normally slept that late. But things weren't normal. A sharp pain shot through her head as she thought of yesterday when she had gone to spy on her ex-husband's wedding.

Her empty stomach rumbled from its depths, but first things first. Despite feeling fragile, Ella went from room to room as quickly as she dared, opening curtains and turning off lights she'd left on the night before. The last thing she wanted was someone knocking on her door checking to make sure everything was alright. This was a small village and people knew each other's ways and schedules. There was probably already more than one well-meaning person keeping an eye on this poor woman whose husband had just re-married right here in the village church.

Ella put the kettle on. The pain was still jabbing at her head as she knelt down to the bottom drawer which held the first aid supplies. She found some aspirin but thought it best to eat something first. Fruit juice would be too acidic for her already griping stomach and just the thought of cereal with creamy milk was beginning to make her retch. She opened the fridge and looked inside and was surprised to see things there she didn't usually buy. Her mind was obviously elsewhere at the time she was shopping. There was some Chorizo sausage. She hated Chorizo. What on earth was she thinking? Ella picked up the packet; it was familiar. She'd bought it before, many times - for Jon. Jon loved Chorizo.

Ella spotted a couple more carrier bags left abandoned over by the kitchen table. She remembered wandering around the supermarket yesterday in a daze, her mind not on washing powder and olive oil but on the marriage blessing taking place at two o'clock that afternoon. She emptied the carrier bags onto the worktop. It was like unpacking a Christmas hamper, not knowing what she was going to find next. There was chocolate covered shortbread, a jar of luxury marmalade and some fruit pies – all very nice but not what she would normally buy on her weekly shop. And this was particularly strange, a box of rose and violet chocolates. They were her grandmother's favourite and Ella used to buy them for her at any excuse, not just birthdays and Christmases. But her grandmother had been dead for over five years.

The last item in the bag was a very appetising crusty wholemeal loaf. Ella's thoughts returned to food and five minutes later she was sitting down to a poached egg on toast and a cup of tea.

Physically she felt much better and now she planned to pack the shopping away, load the dishwasher, take a shower and dress. Ella did all these things and then came to a complete standstill. She was good at planning and organising, always had been, and these skills had served as a lifesaver over the last few months. But every now and then she felt totally immobilized, devoid of any energy at all or the will to do anything.

Not knowing what else to do, Ella lay down on her bed looking up at the ceiling trying to clear her mind like it said in her meditation books. 'Clear your head of all thoughts and focus on your breathing or simply let the thoughts wander in and drift away of their own will.' Ella didn't want any thoughts in her head, she knew what they would be and she didn't want them. "Please stop," she whispered. She didn't want to focus on her breathing either. "I don't care if that stops too." Ella closed her eyes which were filling with tears and wondered what it would be like just to fall asleep here on this bed and not wake up. That would be nice. No more thinking. No more planning. No more weddings.

Ella sat up and swung her legs off the side of the bed immediately ashamed of her thoughts. "I need to get out. I need air." She stomped out of the bedroom and headed downstairs for a coat and walking shoes. "So much for my new start; I'm wanting to end it before it's even begun! I must sort myself out."

It was a classic autumn day; bright blue skies and sunshine but with a sharpness in the air that made her think of bonfires and fireworks and other key events that were just around the corner.

As she walked out of her garden and along the lane, Ella spotted her neighbour Kath returning from a walk with her dog. She waved and smiled but carried on her way, reluctant to get caught in a conversation. She left the lane as quickly as she could, veering off into a field, thankful to be hidden by the hedges and trees. She strolled along keeping to the edge of the field and out of sight. Ella took a deep breath, closed her eyes and lifted her face to the sunshine. She loved being outdoors and although there was plenty of beautiful countryside in Gloucestershire, she regretted being so far away from the coast.

Ella could hear voices coming from the roadside and stopped behind a tree. She could see two brightly coloured fleeces through the branches and waited there until the couple had passed. This was getting to be a silly habit, hiding behind trees. It had to stop.

As if on auto-pilot, Ella found herself heading in the direction of the village church. Twelve years ago she and Jon had married in a church similar to this one. Ella smiled as she remembered her bridesmaids, a cousin who was only four years old and Colette, Jon's daughter from a previous relationship who was a teenager at the time.

Confetti still lay scattered over the ground, piling into the corners of the church doorway and on the steps leading down from the lych gate. In her mind Ella could see Jon, as he was yesterday with his arm around that girl, Danielle. She couldn't even bear to think of her name. She could see the way he looked at her. Ella remembered that look but she couldn't remember when exactly it had stopped for her. And yet they had been so in love. Hadn't they? What had happened?

A car pulled up nearby and an elderly couple got out. Ella was relieved she didn't recognise them but they smiled at her as they passed on their way inside the church. Of course, it was nearly time for Evensong. Ella began walking back quickly before anyone else arrived. She took the longer route back which took in the new development of a dozen executive homes on the outskirts of the village. This was where Jon and his new wife were living. She didn't know exactly which house was theirs, it didn't matter, she wouldn't be popping a Christmas card through their letterbox. It was bad enough they were staying in the village at all.

It was dark by the time Ella arrived back home and the house was freezing. She got the fire going and put a couple of logs on. This had always been Jon's job although he was never very good at it. Lighting the home fire was a man's job, he had said. They had joked at how it was part of his hunter-gatherer instinct. Ella was surprised and relieved to discover she was actually quite a dab hand at it.

Sunday evenings were particularly difficult since Jon had gone and this one was again stretching out endlessly before her. She perched on the edge of the sofa, glass of red wine in hand, staring into the flames and subconsciously asking for answers. And then one came. She should redecorate - the whole house. That's exactly what she needed - a project. It would be symbolic to signify her new beginning. A fresh start.

Ella loved this old house and Jon understood. He'd been very reasonable in the divorce settlement making it possible for her to continue living there. Together they'd found this, their dream house, and put in an offer which was accepted immediately. It had all been very straightforward and problem free. It was things like that, seamlessly falling into place as if they were meant to be, that made it so difficult for Ella to believe it was all over. How had everything so wonderful gone so horribly wrong?

She had hoped she would live the rest of her life in this house but she never imagined she'd be living here on her own. Initially she thought the four large bedrooms and the attic would provide plenty of space to fill with children. She remembered the bombshell when Jon had said he wasn't keen to have any more. It was as though he were saying he wasn't keen on cheese on toast or he wasn't keen on painting the kitchen yellow - as if something else would do instead. Ella had been devastated at the time but told herself that they were both still young and had plenty of time. People change, they mature and mellow and different priorities come into force. Even up until just a few weeks before Jon left, she was still clinging to the hope that maybe a miraculous innocent accident would change their lives.

Of course, Ella questioned how they had got to know each other so intimately, had had a long engagement, planned their wedding and all aspects of their lives without ever discussing children. For her part, she had just assumed they both wanted the same thing. Apparently, Jon had done the same.

Ella struggled to think back to the baby arguments - is that when things had begun to go wrong? She closed her eyes, trying to visualise the scenes and recall conversations. What had been said in anger or reason? She couldn't remember. She contemplated how a relationship destroys itself. Maybe for some, in one dramatic no going back event. But for many, it's the chipping away in tiny increments, so subtle and fine as to go unnoticed for years until it's much too late. The misery, on looking back, to realise you still don't even know where you went wrong and that you can't say you've learnt from your lessons, was almost as despairing.

Ella had been staring, unblinking into the fire for too long and her eyes were stinging and watering. She mentally planned the evening ahead, scheduling each event into neat time slots. Dinner in about half an hour. Clear away kitchen things and load dishwasher. Hot bath perhaps with another glass of wine. There was a film starting at nine-thirty that was nothing to do with romance or broken hearts and perhaps she would even try some of those violet and rose chocolates, which would take her up to almost midnight when it would be time for bed and she could sleep, forget, and hope tomorrow would be an easier day.

Chapter Two

"Hello Ella dear. How are you love? I've been ringing you all morning. Is everything ok?"

Ella knew she couldn't avoid the calls forever. "Hi Kath, I'm fine, thanks. Sorry I didn't hear the phone. I was cleaning, you know, upstairs."

"Good idea – to keep busy I mean. I was worried you might be a bit maudlin about Saturday and everything. I popped along to the church and it all seemed to go ok. If you want to talk anytime, you know where I am."

"Thanks but I'm fine, really."

"Good. Listen, you haven't seen Mardley have you?"

"No, sorry, I haven't." Mardley was Kath's aging but still very lively Labrador. Ella was relieved to change the subject. "He's wandered off has he?"

"Yes, the little monster's left me again." Kath cringed at her bad choice of words and the two-second delay in conversation suggested the apology that was just about to follow. But Ella was getting used to people putting their foot in it and intercepted swiftly.

"Listen Kath, I've got to go. There's someone at the door."

"Oh ok. I'll leave you to it. But remember, if you want to talk I'm only next door."

Ella made herself a mug of black coffee and slumped into the armchair, still in her pyjamas. She thought she'd heard the phone ringing somewhere in her distant consciousness and finally, on the third attempt, it had woken her up. She wished now that she hadn't answered it. Kath would probably find some excuse to pop over just so they could gossip about the wedding. Most of the village were probably doing that already. Why doesn't she just mind her own business, nosey old busybody, thought Ella, immediately feeling guilty. Kath was a good woman at heart. She'd lived in the village all her life, knew everyone and pretty much all their business and saw no reason for that to change.

Kath had noticed Jon staying away from home more frequently and also that his trips were getting progressively longer. It was a while later before Ella even admitted these truths to herself and some considerable time after the event before she could admit to her neighbour that Jon had gone. Admittedly, Kath could have been a very good friend, if Ella had let her.

Ella jumped at the sound of mad scratching at the front door and knew instantly that on the other side there'd be one crazy dog, trying to jump up and barking at her as if they'd been parted for years.

"Hello Mardley, you stupid thing!" Ella knelt down with the intention of trying to calm the Labrador but she was unable to resist giving his soft coat a vigorous ruffle. She rubbed his ears which only got him all the more excited.

"Now what do I do with you?" Ella's first instinct was to walk the dog the short distance along the country lane back to his owner. "I'm not about to go stomping around in my pyjamas, that's for sure. That really would start some rumours. I suppose you'll have to come in for a moment but you'd better behave." She led him by the collar through the lounge quickly before he took a liking to one of the big comfy sofas. In the kitchen she managed to dial Kath's number while still holding on to Mardley's collar. He was trying to break free so they could play.

"Hi Kath. I have something here that belongs to you. Your wandering dog has returned."

"The rascal! I'd almost given up on him."

"Do you want to come over? I'll put the kettle on," she said kindly.

Kath was delighted. "That'll be lovely. I'm on my way."

Ella was conscious of an article she had to get finished by the end of the week. As a freelance journalist it was a great advantage to be able to work from home but sometimes, without the discipline of a nine to five office environment, it was difficult to motivate herself even with a looming deadline. She hadn't even started the article but it suddenly felt more important, at this moment, to spend a little time and show a little kindness to her well-meaning neighbour.

Ella had just a few minutes to change out of her nightclothes before Kath arrived. She also wanted to clean away the evidence from another evening spent over-indulging resulting in her falling asleep on the sofa again. She looked around the kitchen for something to hand which would keep Mardley occupied while she dashed upstairs but she couldn't find anything.

"Right, you stay here and think long and hard before you chew anything."

Ella ran up the stairs, two at a time. She pulled on her jeans and was about to put on a cashmere crew neck sweater when she remembered she was supposed to have been cleaning and so she dashed into the bathroom, had a quick rummage in the laundry basket, and retrieved a crumpled t-shirt. She twisted her long thick hair into a knot and secured it with a clip.

Back downstairs Mardley was lying on the floor on his belly. He looked up as Ella walked in and the bored expression on his face made her laugh. She sat down which was a cue for Mardley to join her for some serious stroking and fussing, just as Kath tapped on the window of the back door before letting herself in.

Ella got up and Kath sat down taking over petting duties with Mardley, showing she was pleased to see him while at the same time giving him a good telling off for disappearing in the first place.

Ella made coffee while quickly clearing away last night's dinner things hoping Kath wouldn't notice. One empty wine bottle was placed swiftly in the bin while the half empty one was tucked away in the corner. She placed the mugs on a tray and an assortment of biscuits on a plate.

"Shall we have these outside? It looks quite warm out there, might as well make the most of the sunshine."

"Good idea. It's a little fresh but you're right, let's make the most of it. There you go Mardley, have a run around the garden and you can come back for a biscuit." Mardley took off towards the end of the huge garden as though he'd never seen open ground before.

"So, you're ok are you?" asked Kath.

Ella fidgeted and took a bite of her biscuit. "Mm, I'm fine thanks, really."

"Good girl. You're putting all this behind you and getting on with your life. This is the closing of a chapter that's all. And a new one is about to begin. You'll see. That's how it goes in life."

Ella felt tears prick the back of her eyes. To hear Kath speak so casually about getting on with her life made her despair. All she was doing was getting through each day. Ella felt all her good intentions to be neighbourly slip away. She didn't feel like talking now but fortunately Kath could sense it.

The old woman glanced across at Ella; tall and slim, not too skinny like a lot of silly girls today, she thought. She had a perfect complexion; healthy and rosy cheeked from enjoying the outdoor life and the most beautiful long dark hair. What sort of a stupid man would want to walk away from a woman like Ella? Kath unknowingly shook her head, acknowledging to herself that she was losing her understanding on the ways of the world.

They sat for a while longer in silence and then made the occasional comment about the garden and the changing season. All Ella could think of was the dark, cold nights and everything dying.

"Right, I'm going to attempt to round up my wretched dog and give him a good bath since I don't know exactly where he's been all morning. Thanks for the coffee, love. Bye for now, you take care." Kath stood to go but couldn't resist a final comment. She bent down close to Ella's ear, tapped her lightly on the shoulder with one finger and whispered as if this would take the harshness out of her words. "You're better off without him. You're well rid. Believe me." She walked off down the garden path still pointing her finger in the air. Ella continued to sit outside for a while even though she was getting cold, Kath's words suspended in her mind.

Jon worked for a large pharmaceutical company and had recently been promoted to Director in Business Development. It was something he'd worked hard for and Ella remembered how happy he'd been at the promotion.

She reflected on happy times with suspicion now, never quite sure of the real source of his happiness. They used to celebrate all sorts of little niceties; the booking of a holiday, the delivery of the Aga and even the first blossoming of the rose tree they'd planted at the end of the drive – any excuse to open the bubbly. They hadn't done anything to celebrate Jon's promotion and at the time Ella thought it a little odd but dismissed it. He was so caught up with the arrangements for his first business trip to Japan. Now, of course, she could guess who he'd celebrated with.

Jon's new job involved a lot of travel all over the world. Ella tried to keep up with it all. She would make notes in her diary of where he was going and when he was coming back. She offered him lifts to and from the airport whenever she could but it wasn't long before it all started to get muddled. There were always so many last minute changes and then there were trips she didn't even know about until the day before even though Jon was adamant he had told her about them.

There was no one dramatic defining moment, no receipt for fancy underwear found in a trouser pocket, or sighting of him by a friend in a backstreet restaurant. The business trips just became more frequent and impromptu. Ella would come down in the morning and if Jon's case was by the front door, she knew he would be leaving that morning. Tentatively she would ask when he was coming back and was simply relieved when he gave an answer.

On reflection the silent signs were screaming at her but she wasn't ready to hear them at the time. Ella calculated the day. It was almost exactly eight months ago. Early spring. Everything beginning anew and coming to life. The day her marriage ended.

Ella came downstairs one Saturday morning as usual. Jon was already up even though he'd been pottering about with something or other well into the early hours. As Ella descended into the hallway she noticed Jon's luggage by the front door. She'd learned to judge from the luggage he took, how long he'd be away. The small holdall meant between one and three nights whereas the larger wheelie suitcase could mean anything up to two weeks at a time. But here on the floor, stacked up neatly and precisely, was the whole set of their matching luggage.

Jon gently threw his raincoat on top. He looked at Ella, his eyes acknowledging the hurt he was causing.

"You're not coming back, are you?"

"No," he whispered.

Ella hurried passed into the kitchen. "I hope you don't mind if I don't give you a lift to the airport," she called out. She was leaning heavily against the sink, the cold ceramic gripped with both her hands. She felt it dig hard into her ribs as her breathing quickened into short uncontrollable gasps.

Jon was standing in the doorway.

"Ella, I –."

"Just go. Please, just go." Ella couldn't turn to look at him. She couldn't even speak his name. She heard the front door open and after he'd placed the luggage outside, he gently closed it again.

She looked into the sink, glaring at the plughole intently, studying its circle of holes. She wanted to be sick into it but with no food in her belly all she could do was retch in painful spasms, knowing full well this was only the start of it.

Chapter Three

The phone rang early. It was probably Kath. Ella was busy and she hoped Mardley hadn't escaped again.

"Hi Ella, it's Colette. Sorry, I know it's early. I wanted to get you before I left for work. How are you?"

"Hello Colette. It's lovely to hear from you. God, it's atrocious weather here. The rain woke me this morning so don't worry, I've been up for ages. I'm ok, been working hard over the last few weeks, got back in touch with some editors, you know, let them know I'm still alive."

Colette was Jon's daughter, pretty and petite, a young woman now in her twenties. Jon had met Colette's mother while at university, they hadn't been together long before she fell pregnant but she was adamant she would keep the baby and dropped out of university as well as Jon's life to devote herself to motherhood. Initially, Jon just kept in touch for the sake of doing the right thing but inevitably he'd grown to love his baby daughter and when he married Ella, she too had been captivated by the sweet little girl.

"Anyway, how's everything with you?" asked Ella.

Colette knew her voice sounded flat. Ella was doing a much better job of pretending that everything was fine and rosy. "I'm good. Weather's bad here too. Listen, is it ok if I come up tomorrow? Simon's away on some business trip and not back until Saturday. Could I stop at yours for the night and we could spend some time together?"

"Of course you can, anytime. But listen Colette, I am fine, really. There's no need for you to be checking up on me or anything. I've had a rough few weeks, sulked like a teenager and drank too much wine but I'm coming out of it now. So don't you go worrying on my account, ok?"

"I'm glad you're alright. But really, I would like to come and see you. So tomorrow's ok? We could go for lunch or something."

"Sounds lovely, perfect actually. I'm really looking forward to it."

Ella was glad that her relationship with Colette was not affected by Jon's leaving or by his re-marrying. She got stuck into her work, carrying on well into the evening so that she could be fully free the next day. She finally finished a couple of articles and got half a dozen proposals together ready to be posted. That night Ella slept deep and peacefully and awoke feeling refreshed and looking forward to the day.

The first thing was to get the guest bedroom ready. Ella enjoyed all that sort of thing; getting out the pretty bed linen, soft cotton sheets decorated with delicate embroidery and arranging fresh flowers from the garden in a vase on the dressing table.

There was still plenty of time before Colette arrived and Ella was going from room to room tweaking ornaments in place and straightening curtains, unable to sit still. She looked out the window along the lane. It was still raining heavily and she hoped the bad weather wouldn't delay her step-daughter.

Ella couldn't bear the idea of spending the next couple of hours fidgeting and twitching. She needed to find something else to do and decided to bake some bread. How welcoming it would be for Colette to arrive to the warm, comforting smell of homemade bread baking in the oven.

Now there was no stopping her; Ella was on a mission to present a vision of perfect country comfort, just for fun. She popped a couple of part-baked baguettes in the oven and then changed the tablecloth on the kitchen table for a pure linen one adorned with a lavish lace hem and then she set the table with some fine china. Colette would love it.

Finally, Ella stood back and admired her efforts. The bread smelled gorgeous already. She opened the oven door and peeked inside, the baguettes were just beginning to brown nicely. She turned the temperature down to prolong the aroma.

Ella heard the sound of swishing tyres on wet tarmac outside and dashed to open the door, holding it open as Colette parked high on the drive as near to the house as she could. She ran the short distance to the house, still getting soaked on the way. Ella stood aside to let her in, eager to give her a big hug but waiting patiently while she took off her jacket. She noticed Colette was looking tired and pale.

"Come here then," Ella put her arms around the young woman. "It's lovely to see you." Colette had her in what felt like a bear hug, as if she didn't want to let go. Finally she pulled back, avoiding eye contact.

"Is everything ok?" Ella asked, willing the answer to be a yes. She didn't think she could cope with anyone else's problems, not at the moment. She just wanted a nice day.

"Yes. Fine."

"Mm, it doesn't sound like it to me. Come on through to the kitchen and I'll put the kettle on."

Colette stopped in mid track and put her face in her hands. "Oh Ella!"

All the excitement of Colette's visit was beginning to drain away and Ella fought to cling to her high spirits of the morning. "What's wrong Collie? Come on, it can't be that bad, eh? Come through to the kitchen and we can talk."

Ella led the way eager for Colette to see what she'd been up to all morning but the lacy tablecloth and pretty china didn't have the same uplifting effect they had earlier on. Colette sat down at the table not even noticing Ella's efforts carried out in her honour.

Ella spoke quietly now. "What's wrong? What's happened?"

Colette rubbed her forehead, the action of a weary woman much older than her twenty-five years. She sighed. "Nothing's really wrong. And nothing's really happened. Not like anything awful. Not like anyone getting ill or dying or anything."

"Ok, well that's good. But what then? Something's up."

"It's to do with Dad. And Danielle."

Ella felt her chest muscles constrict as her heart beat faster and her stomach churned. She didn't want this anymore. She wanted to move on, she was trying hard to move on.

"Look Colette, I don't want to sound rude. You and me are always going to have your father in common but he has chosen his life and really that now has nothing to do with me." She was sounding much braver than she felt. "Don't feel obliged to fill me in on every little detail of his life. I certainly don't expect you to. You're not being disloyal to me - in fact, I don't even want to know what he's up to. The less I know the better. There, you see, I'm ok about everything. Really."

"No, listen Ella. This isn't just a little detail. This is kind of big. And everyone is going to know pretty soon. And I just think you'd rather hear from me, probably, rather than just anyone. You see, what it is - they're going to have a baby."

Ella wasn't entirely sure she hadn't blacked out for a couple of seconds. Colette fetched a glass of water. "Here, drink this. Or should you have something stronger? Brandy. Do you have some brandy?"

Ella wasn't really listening. She wanted to rewind the last few minutes of her life, delete the bit that said her ex-husband was about to start a family with someone else – rewrite the script and fast forward to Colette visiting, make it all nice with warm bread and melted butter, pretty china and everything being alright.

She sipped the water. It made her feel sick. Nothing would ever, ever be alright.

"Are you ok?" Colette didn't know what else she could say. She leaned forward and tucked a loose strand of hair away from Ella's face. "You have nice hair. You should leave it loose sometimes." Colette turned slightly and sniffed the air. "Ella, I think something's burning."

"Mm?"

"Shall I have a look?"

"Yes. Please."

Colette removed the bread from the oven. And then she noticed how pretty the kitchen looked and finally realised how much effort Ella had gone to, to make everything look lovely. And now it was all spoilt. And the bread was burnt.

The following morning, after a sleepless night, Colette had already been up for a while. They hadn't managed to get out for their lunch yesterday. Ella had been far too distraught. Colette had known that the news would come as a terrible blow but even she hadn't reckoned on Ella reacting this bad. Ella had confided in her a few years earlier. She'd explained that she'd wanted children of her own but Jon hadn't wanted any more. And so Colette understood fully the hopeless sadness in Ella's eyes as well as her intense anger.

But now she wanted to get back home so she'd be there when Simon returned but as yet she hadn't heard a sound from Ella's room. She couldn't possibly just leave her, not after last night. They had both had a lot to drink. It was as if Ella had been on a mission to block everything out.

Colette made a cup of tea and tapped lightly on the door. Nothing. She knocked harder and opened the door a little, and for one iota of a second panicked at what she might find on the other side. She was physically relieved at the sight of Ella turning to face her.

"Good morning sleepy head. Here, I brought you a cup of tea."

"Oh god. Is it morning already? What time is it?"

"It's just after ten. But I need to be going soon. Shall I just slip off, leave you to have a bit of a lie-in?"

"No, no. Don't be daft, I'm getting up."

"Ok, I'll see you downstairs."

Colette paced a little, listening to the sound of Ella moving around clumsily upstairs. It had been a heavy evening, as she knew it would be. She had never seen Ella so distraught; she had sobbed miserably one minute and then ranted against her father the next. She remembered it all quite vividly and hoped that perhaps Ella's memory wouldn't be so clear. Finally she appeared in the kitchen.

"I hope I look better than I feel although I know I don't."

"You look fine, really."

"Mm, you're just being kind." Ella began filling the kettle.

"I've made tea already," said Colette, sitting down at the kitchen table. Ella joined her, sighed, closed her eyes and rested her head in her hand.

"Listen Collie, I hope I wasn't too much of a pain last night." It was such an effort to talk. She could remember crying while Colette hugged her. She thought maybe she had said some awful things about Colette's father but wasn't sure if she'd only thought them.

"It's ok Ella, really. Let's just forget it."

"No, I have to apologise. None of this is your fault. It isn't fair on you."

"I came here to tell you this news. Remember? I knew you'd be upset. That's why I came. It isn't the sort of thing I could send by text message, is it?"

Ella gave a weak smile, knowing lesser people would have done. "You're a very good person, with a mature head on your young shoulders." Ella suddenly felt very old.

"Ella, I don't want us to drift apart. Ever. I want us to stay friends. I don't care what happens between Dad and -." Colette lowered her voice to a whisper as if it was all she had the energy for. "I just want us to stay the same."

Ella nodded in agreement, unable to speak. She suddenly realised how difficult the last couple of days must have been for Colette.

"I love you like a second Mum, Ella. And I know, I know, you're nowhere near old enough to be my mother - but you know what I mean."

"Mm," is all Ella could manage without completely breaking down. She took Colette's hand in hers and despite her best efforts, still one or two tears managed to escape and trickle down her cheek.

Colette could hear the muffled ring of her mobile in her handbag and reluctantly freed her hand from Ella's.

"Hi Simon."

"Hi Col. Where are you, with Ella? Is she alright?"

"Yeah, where are you, at the airport yet?"

"No, I'm home. I got an earlier flight. You ok?"

"Yes, I'm fine. I'll be leaving soon."

Colette and Simon had been together for just over two years and were renting a flat in north London, near enough to both their families but still in the thick of city life. Colette longed to be back there now, with Simon.

"Ella, I'd better get going. Simon's back early. Will you be ok?"

"Of course I will. You get on your way."

"I don't like leaving you like this."

"I'll be fine. I'll get my head together - probably quicker if I'm on my own for a while. You know what I mean. I'll be ok. You're not to worry about me."

"But I do. I knew this would be a shock. I'll phone you tonight. And you'd better pick up. If I get your bloody answer machine, I'll be driving straight back up here, ok?" Colette was training to be a nursery school teacher. With her sense of organisation, genuine caring nature, and a bit of bossiness, Ella thought she would be brilliant at it.

Ella smiled. "Ok. Now get going or you'll have no weekend left with Simon."

The house was cold. Ella went into the lounge, sat on the edge of the sofa, sorted a couple of logs from the basket and reached out for the firelighters. But then she changed her mind. A roaring fire would make no difference. She would still feel like ice inside. Ella acknowledged her failing. Despite sneaking off to witness her ex-husband's wedding, she hadn't been able to let him go, she still loved him and had believed he might come back. Throughout the divorce proceedings, when they were both polite and pleasant to each other, she thought at any moment he might change his mind. Even when the envelope arrived with the Decree Absolute, she consoled herself with the fact that it wasn't unusual for divorced couples to remarry. And even a couple of days before the wedding, a noise at the front door late at night had her running down the stairs, frantically unlocking the door, convinced Jon would be standing on the other side. But there had been no-one there.

Now a definitive shift had occurred. And there was definitely no going back from this. She began thinking about her decorating plans. It didn't feel like such a good idea anymore. She couldn't recapture her earlier enthusiasm. No amount of redecorating or bright colours would bring this house back to life for her. And it was so quiet, with Jon gone and now Colette gone. She didn't think she could bear the quietness of this big house any longer.

Ella sat slumped on the sofa, head in her hands. She wanted to cry but had no tears left. She realised what she really wanted was to run away – as far as possible. Immediately she thought of her beloved little beach hut. She could easily camp out there for a few days.

The hut had originally belonged to her grandparents and had been passed down through the family. Ella smiled as she remembered happy, carefree childhood holidays on the beautiful Hampshire coast with her parents. She recalled trips to Southsea Castle and taking a tour from Portsmouth Harbour on the waterbus. Being an only child, everything had been centred on her and she had had great fun. The cosy beach hut was a home from home, providing all the comforts but with the added excitement of being exposed to the mercy of the elements. It had been a place of sanctuary too. Both her parents died while she was studying journalism at university and it was to the beach hut she bolted every weekend for months afterwards, partly to be alone with her grief but also because she felt close to them there. She had imagined taking her own children to the beach hut and doing the same things with them; poking about in rock pools, playing ball games in the sun and then getting wrapped up in woollies and wellies and going for long deserted beach walks in the winter.

The idea of a change of scene seemed so right to her in that instant but she also knew that a few days at the beach hut wouldn't be enough. Suddenly she smiled, she couldn't live in her beach hut long term, but it would be a dream come true to live nearer to it and that whole way of life right on the coast, near the beaches and the sea.

Ella stood up as if to salute the massive decision she had just made. She had decided to sell her house and move far away where hopefully she really could make a new start.

Chapter Four

Libby and the other ladies bustled into Charles de Gaulle airport with just enough time to check in, only to discover their flight to Heathrow was delayed.

There was a lot of moaning and watch consulting but Libby didn't mind too much, there wasn't anything particular to rush home for. The children would be on their week-end stay with their father and a neighbour would have called by earlier in the day to feed the cats and walk the dogs.

The ladies had been to Paris for a day trip. They'd spent the morning at the Louvre; fiercely debating the merits, or not, of the glass pyramid entrance in the main courtyard. Then they'd gone on for lunch and spent the rest of the afternoon shopping. It had been a long day, setting off for the airport at six-thirty in the morning and then having to take two trains to get into the centre of Paris. It would be at least a couple of hours more before they were home and the group of women sat, tired and worn out, in agitated silence.

Francine broke the atmosphere. "Shall we go get a drink?" Everyone agreed this was a good idea and collectively gathered their bags and packages before moving over to the bar area in the lounge. Libby made an effort to position herself next to Francine so she could thank her for today's invite. She'd had a fantastic time but the competition was too great and Francine was soon flanked on either side by women who were much quicker off the mark than Libby.

Francine was organising the drinks order. Libby asked for a dry white wine, Francine deliberated for a second or two and then ordered a Cointreau. Libby wished she'd done the same.

Perched high on her bar stool, Libby cast an admiring glance over her friend; tall and slim, she was elegantly dressed in caramel wool trousers, and a cream cashmere sweater, a lightweight shawl in a flattering shade of apricot was stylishly draped around her shoulders. Libby envied her perfect style. She had been slim once but that was many years ago before she had the children and even though they were in their teens now, she had never been able to regain her trim figure.

Libby sipped her wine and thought about all the nice things and gifts she had bought including a box of those lovely macaroons in all their pretty colours. They were expensive but she managed to convince herself they were bound to be worth it. Their little group was completely surrounded by fancy boutique bags and Libby wondered how much money had been spent during their one day in Paris. She knew she might not be able to keep up with them for much longer but she dismissed the thought quickly before it could spoil her day.

Libby didn't know any of these women, they were all friends of Francine's and various conversations were going on around her. She tuned into one closest to her.

"It's such a shame Elizabeth couldn't make it. We've all been looking forward to it for so long and then the poor thing breaks her ankle the day before."

"Yes, it is," said another woman who turned and touched Libby gently on her arm. "It's a good job you could make it at such short notice."

"Yes, I suppose it is," said Libby trying not to look too disappointed. She had thought the trip to Paris was a spur of the moment thing. She wasn't aware she was the substitute.

"Oh well, at least she'll be fine by the time we do the next one," said the first lady. "Francine was talking about New York for a few days. I like the idea of that."

So do I, thought Libby, wondering if she would be invited. She hoped she would be.

They were due to board soon and Libby slipped carefully off her stool to go to the ladies' room. A group of long legged flight attendants briskly walked passed, smart and efficient, pulling their compact wheelie cases behind them. Libby felt short and dumpy as they marched by, their high heels clicking on the polished floor. She had been a flight attendant, or airhostess as they used to be called, many years ago. It was a good time in her life and she liked to talk about it – even though it now felt like a hundred years ago. She glanced sideways at the group of fresh, young faces, expertly made up with their hair perfectly styled into place. She wondered if she had ever looked as good in the job.

Inside the ladies' room, Libby looked at her reflection while washing her hands. She wasn't impressed at the flushed round face looking back at her. Her favourite pink lipstick made her look pale rather than glamorous and despite liking her highlighted blonde hair, she thought the short bob and heavy fringe were maybe a little old fashioned now.

Most of the ladies nodded off on the hour long flight home. Libby had a window seat and at first she thought she was the only one awake until she looked across the aisle and saw Francine flicking through a glossy magazine. It was a shame they were seated apart, she thought, they could have had a nice little chat and got to know each other better if they had been sitting together. She stared at Francine for some time, knowing she couldn't be seen.

With no hold luggage to collect, they passed through security quickly and gathered together again outside the terminal at the taxi rank. Tired now, Libby observed the group as they sprang into action, animatedly debating who lived nearer to who and who should share which taxis. It took a while for them to realise ten women would not fit into one vehicle with Francine and further debate ensued as to who had priority. Those who drew the short straws got into other taxis, huffy and disappointed. Libby shivered in the cold autumn evening and quickly got into a taxi by herself, just looking forward to getting home now.

Libby's was the biggest house high up on the lane with the best view of the coastline below and even though it couldn't be seen this late at night, she felt safe just knowing the boundary of the beach was out there and the sea beyond. She walked up the drive, across the garden and entered through the kitchen at the back. The outside security light came on automatically, lighting up the beautifully landscaped garden. The house itself was in darkness until Libby switched on a small brass lamp on the window cill giving a soft warm glow to the large kitchen, clean and pristinely organised.

Friday was Mrs O'Brien's day for coming in and cleaning. Libby loved Fridays; everything fresh, clean and tidy. She appreciated it even more on weekends like this when the children were with their Dad; the house had a better chance of staying tidy for a while - at least until they returned on Sunday evening. Libby looked around, inspecting Mrs O'Brien's efforts and nodding in approval. She tweaked the bottle of hand-wash back to where it should be and draped the kitchen cloth over the side of the sink rather than hanging it over the tap as Mrs O'Brien always did.

Libby went through to the lounge and chose a relaxing CD, altering the settings so the music would be piped into her bedroom and the en suite bathroom. She adjusted the volume down from the deafening rock concert level which one of her children had set it at and then took her bags and parcels upstairs and plonked them on the bed before running a bath. She took out a long sleeved t-shirt she'd bought for Jess. It was black. Everything had to be black. Jess was sixteen. The t-shirt had a sequined Eiffel Tower on the front which she hoped didn't clash with any of the current fashion dictates for sixteen year old girls.

Todd, at seventeen, was much more difficult to buy for. She'd bought him a book at The Louvre on the history of art. Todd was in his final year of GCSEs and was studying art although Libby wasn't overly keen on what she'd seen so far. He was into black too and greys with the odd splodge of red. Did that represent blood? She wondered. She tried to be encouraging but really she had no idea what his work was about.

After a hot bath, Libby nestled into her big bed. She loved the smell of fresh sheets Mrs O'Brien had put on. She glanced at the brand new hardback on the bedside table waiting to be opened and reached for the large glass of good white wine and took a sip, sinking back against the pillows. Libby felt satisfied and content with her day but was also wondering where things would go from here with her new friends. Would Francine invite her to New York? And if she did, would she still be able to go by then?

Chapter Five

"Good morning Miss Peters."

"Hi there Steve, still no interest in my house? I've not had one viewing yet. Should I be getting worried?"

"It's early days. And the market is a little slow still."

"I know. But I want a quick sale. I think it's overpriced – I'm thinking I should reduce it by, maybe, fifty thousand."

"Come in, take a seat. Let's see what we can do." Ella stayed where she was near the open doorway. "I'm sorry Steve, I don't have time for a long discussion right now. I just want to move things along."

"They're predicting an upturn in a couple of months or so."

"I can't wait that long. I'm lucky; I can afford to drop my price. If the market is slow, as you say, I need to do something drastic now before it's too late. Fifty thousand, I want to drop it by fifty thousand. Will you do that today Steve, please?"

"Ok, Miss Peters, if that's what you want. If you're absolutely sure. I'll do it today, change it on the website and amend the ad going out in tomorrow's locals."

"Thanks Steve. That's great. Much appreciated."

Shortly after visiting the estate agent while Ella was shopping, she took a call on her mobile. It was Steve phoning to tell her about a couple who wanted to view her house - that evening if possible. Ella went straight home to clean and tidy her already clean and tidy house.

The couple arrived on time and Ella gave them a mental thumbs up as they walked through the door, wiping their feet and casting admiring glances at the décor. They were looking for something bigger than their present three-bedroom semi as they needed more room for their expanding family of three school age children and a fourth on the way.

That is how it should be, Ella thought. A big rambling house like this should be filled with a large, noisy family, not a mid-thirties divorcee rattling around in it getting more and more bitter with the advancing years.

Ella led the way as they moved from room to room. Sometimes the couple were completely bowled over by a specific feature, an original fireplace or a particular view of the garden, and at other times they were silent and contemplative. Ella smiled, despite herself, at their chatter debating which child would want which bedroom. She tried to give positive answers to their questions but she wasn't about to be deceitful in her attempt to sell her house. The electric wiring needed some updating and no amount of positivity could hide the fact that the roof needed a few repairs.

When the viewing was over, Ella felt completely deflated. She was unable to read the situation. She resigned herself to a long and frustrating wait before knowing the outcome. She wandered from room to room, unable to settle her body or mind. Her thoughts were vacillating between wanting a quick sale and an uncomfortable feeling about it all; the intrusion of strangers inspecting her home, her private world, to see if it was good enough for them. Ella tried to imagine this lively family living here but she struggled with the images. For the first time since she had put her house on the market, she was beginning to doubt she was doing the right thing.

At eight-thirty the following morning Ella received a phone call from Steve, the estate agent. The couple had put in an offer for her house at the original full asking price.

"I take it you'll accept Miss Peters?"

"Yes. Of course, my god, I can't believe it. This is such a surprise."

"You wanted a quick sale, didn't you?"

"Well, yes I did, but –"

"And as I said, this is at the original asking price. I took this call yesterday, just after you called by. I got the strong impression your house is exactly what these people have been looking for."

Ella was in shock. This was amazing, such a quick sale. Provided nothing went wrong, of course, she reminded herself. She hoped nothing would go wrong and despite her misgivings last night, she now had an overwhelming feeling this was the right thing for her.

The whole process had gone without a hitch and here she was, middle of February, surrounded by boxes and various piles of her things. One pile was labelled for the charity shop, one for keeping, one for throwing out and another pile was for things she couldn't make up her mind about. This last pile seemed to be growing bigger all the time. Ella started off bold and ruthless, throwing away photos and ornaments and the following day, feeling more sentimental, she would retrieve the items and place them on the keep or the don't know pile. She was convinced everything had been in every pile at least once and probably many times over. It felt like she was playing pass-the-parcel with all her stuff just going round and round in endless circles.

Finally she decided to just pack everything and sort it at the other end. Hopefully her head would be clearer by then. And besides her new home was a little old cottage, much smaller than this place and anything that didn't fit would simply have to go.

Ella watched the removal lorry drive away. All she had to do now was to put the last few things in her car and set off for the coast and her new life.

This was the part Ella was dreading; the final good-bye. In no hurry now, she climbed the stairs up to the top floor of the house, intending to say good-bye to each room in turn.

The attic rooms were full of historic atmosphere and although they'd only ever been used for storage, Ella had had great plans for them. She replayed the images of nurseries decorated in pink and blue with musical mobiles hanging from the ceilings and shelves overflowing with storybooks. But she acknowledged these were outdated memories now, as old and dusty as the bare wooden floorboards. Ella plodded down to the first floor. The master bedroom and her office no longer held any attachment for her now they were empty of all her furnishings and personal things. They were just that - empty rooms, ready to be filled with different things and different memories by different people.

As she descended the stairs back down into the hall, the sight of the bare rooms caused a sudden stab of memory back to when she and Jon were moving in all those years ago. The excitement of a new chapter beginning in their lives kept them up until the early hours on their first night, eager to unpack favourite items and see them in their new surroundings. She felt none of that old excitement now. Ella sighed as she symbolically closed the living room door and then the dining room door before going into the kitchen, lingering over finally leaving the last room behind. She wanted to be brave and say she didn't need this house. Everything she possessed was heading off down the road a few miles ahead and what happened next in her life wasn't dependent on the building she lived in, it was dependent upon only herself. But the gut wrenching reality was she couldn't imagine never coming back here ever again. She tidied the various instruction manuals into a neat pile, placing the list of useful phone numbers on top. There was nothing else to do, she fiddled with the house keys that she had to leave behind, her other hand clasped to her mouth to stifle a sudden sob. She stood there for a minute or so, unable to send the final instruction to her brain to get her legs moving towards the front door for the last time.

Ella took a deep breath and placed the keys back on the worktop with some finality then lifted the last small box in the hallway and tucked it under her arm. She pulled the front door shut behind her and drove away, a constant stream of tears gently trickling down her cheeks.

Monday afternoon and Libby still felt happy and relaxed after her weekend. The children had arrived home Sunday evening tired and worn out after an active weekend with their Dad. They were so tired they went to bed early not even allowing themselves time to make a mess.

Libby looked up at the clock; they should've been home from school by now. Instinctively, she walked through to the conservatory that spanned almost the entire side of the house. From here, she had a panoramic view of the beach below and the sea beyond. Libby looked along the lane towards the narrow steep steps leading down to the beach. The children usually took a shortcut across the beach and even though Libby had made it a rule that they were to come straight home from school, they had taken to dawdling with their friends and hanging around the beach huts for a while. What Libby wanted was for them to come home first so she knew they were ok and then let her know where they were going next, with whom and for how long. She was beginning to realise she was expecting a lot from two teenagers.

From the conservatory she had a good view of the whole beach but it was still difficult to pick out her two children amongst the sea of black blazers trimmed with red piping. She swore they only wore their blazers so they would be hidden in the crowd.

Finally she spotted them in the distance to her far right, standing together with some friends by the beach huts. She watched them for a few moments hoping they weren't misbehaving although she had no reason to believe they were. They were both doing well at school, both very active and out in all weathers. They niggled each other; borrowing stuff without asking and teasing over who fancied who but often Libby would catch them deep in conversation, or sharing a joke about something or other. They were good kids and Libby was very proud of them. She was also aware problems could arise out of nowhere and tried to keep close to them, keeping the impossible balance between caring and interfering.

Libby had lost sight of Jess and Todd and then they suddenly appeared at the top of the narrow steps bringing them onto the lane just in front of the house. Libby darted back to the kitchen. She didn't want them to think she'd been spying on them or even worse for them to know she'd been clock watching.

"Hello you two. Good day?"

From the resultant grunts and nods, Libby deduced that today had been another typically uneventful day at school like every other. Libby was just about to comment, unable to stop herself, on why they were a little late home when Todd saved her the trouble.

"Been a fire on the beach," he mumbled.

"Has there? Whereabouts?"

"One of the beach huts."

"Oh, that's awful. How did it start, do they know?"

"Police think it's kids."

Libby looked up from her vegetable chopping.

"Not us! Don't worry!"

"I know. I wasn't worried," said Libby feeling guilty. "What a terrible shame though. Someone's lovely beach hut and all their home from home things inside. It's horrible."

"Nah, it was an empty one," said Todd as if that made it alright.

Libby was just about to ask more about this empty hut; beach huts didn't become available very often. Perhaps he meant one that was closed up for the winter but Todd had already slung his school bag over his shoulder and left the kitchen. Jess quickly followed.

Ella drove hard so she could arrive as soon as possible after the removal lorry. She had half expected to pass the lorry on the motorway in her nippy sports car but as yet, she hadn't seen it. Either the driver was keener than her to get there, or maybe she had passed it already and hadn't noticed.

It was late afternoon by the time she was driving through familiar scenery and it was just beginning to get dark. As she drove along the cliff road which wound round and down steeply, she could see in the distance the welcoming sight of the small beach, nestled in its protective bay. At the far end, looking like a miniature model village from this distance, was the row of beach huts. There were about a dozen of them guarding the shoreline. They weren't lined up in a regimental line like in some coastal resorts but in a higgledy-piggledy row that made them look all the more charming.

She finally descended onto the narrow lane that ran parallel to the beach and arrived outside her new home and drove onto the driveway. The removal lorry was nowhere in sight and she looked around to see if it had parked nearby although the obvious thing would have been to reverse onto the driveway and wait there.

Ella stood, hands on hips, feeling rather conspicuous, looking out towards the main road and willing the lorry to appear along it. She got back into her car and reversed down the drive leaving it free for the lorry and parked on the roadside. She took her handbag and walked up to the cottage, letting herself into her new home for the very first time. Initially it was disappointing that the lorry hadn't yet arrived but now it was actually very nice to have a few minutes in the empty place to herself.

During the drive down, Ella was mindful of the fact that she hadn't seen the property for some weeks and she couldn't exactly recall the proportions of the cottage. As she stepped into the cold empty kitchen, her footsteps echoing noisily on the flagstones, she winced at how small it was. The low ceilings and small windows were such a contrast to the house she had just left behind. But after just a few seconds, she fell in love with it all over again. It felt right to be here, as if she belonged. The cottage dated from the mid 1800s and she wandered from room to room musing over who the first occupants might have been. It still retained many of its original Victorian features Ella loved so much even though the cottage itself had been added to over the years, creating additional rooms on different levels, up a step here and down two steps there. There was even a cellar and the original pantry in the kitchen. She was in there now imagining all her own storage jars and tins stacked neatly on the shelves. Although nothing would be neatly stored anywhere until it arrived - pretty soon hopefully, thought Ella. She went into the lounge at the back of the cottage. It was freezing in here, colder even than outside. She'd lost all sense of time now, had she really been driving so fast she'd managed to get here quicker than the removals people? Perhaps they'd got lost. She decided to give them a call and rummaged in her bag for her phone but couldn't find it. She emptied her bag on the kitchen worktop but still no phone.

"Must have left it in the car. My god! I hope I left it in the car. If I've packed it by mistake -."

Ella ran out to her car, relieved to see her mobile lying on the passenger seat, and she had three missed calls. Someone was keen to get hold of her. She didn't recognise the number and was deliberating over whether to return the call when the number appeared on the screen again.

"Miss Peters?" A very anxious elderly voice spoke at the other end.

"Yes."

"Oh, thank goodness. I've been trying to get hold of you for a while. I'm afraid I have some bad news. The lorry containing your furniture and contents has broken down."

"Oh great! So, how much longer will it be?"

"The mechanic is with them at this moment and he's advised us that a new part has to be ordered but he won't be able to fit it until tomorrow."

"Right. So what happens now? About all my things? What am I supposed to do?"

"I'm very sorry for all the inconvenience."

Ella sighed, trying to think.

"Miss Peters, please book yourself into a hotel for tonight and we'll cover the cost. I'm really very sorry. Is that ok?"

"Yes, thank-you, that's fine. I'll sort something out. And will you let me know in the morning what time the lorry will arrive?"

"Yes, of course."

Looking back towards her cottage, Ella was thinking what to do. She could stay there for the night, although as keen as she was to move in, the thought of sleeping on the floor in the freezing cold – it wasn't really an option. She didn't fancy booking into a hotel either. And then she had an inspired idea. She would stay in her beach hut down on the seafront. It was already her home from home, full of creature comforts and everything she would need for the night. It was the obvious thing to do, the perfect solution. Suddenly the inconvenience of the lorry breaking down turned into a delightfully wicked excuse for a bit of an adventure.

Ella locked up the cottage and made some plans. As she'd been coming here since her childhood, she knew the area well and drove to a local supermarket to get some provisions. She took a trolley from its queue and prepared a mental list of goodies for an evening feast. She felt like a child being allowed to camp out in a tent in the back garden and better still, being allowed to shop for whatever camp-food she wanted.

The picture on the box of the lasagne ready-meal for one looked delicious but just in case the look was deceptive, Ella chose some back-up provisions in the form of an asparagus quiche, sausage rolls and packets of crisps. And then she caught sight of the delicatessen counter and decided to go all out for a one man celebration party, adding coleslaw, olives and a selection of cold meats to her trolley. An assortment of biscuits and cakes and finally some chocolate were piled on top and as Ella decided it really was time to check out, she grabbed a couple of glossy magazines to keep her company.

Ella drove back along the coast road and parked next to her cottage on the roadside. She unloaded her bags from the boot and walked down the narrow steps onto the beach. It was totally dark now, just a few kids hanging around in small groups, but the familiarity of the place prevented her from feeling uneasy. The carrier bags were quite heavy and it was difficult walking over the sand and in the dark with only the light of the moon to guide her. The sand flicked up, over Ella's feet and into her shoes - it was cold and damp. She passed the first couple of beach huts which were raised above the sand on wooden stilts with narrow wooden steps leading up to their doors. The next few huts were sitting on ground level and her one was at the far end, the last but one. As she approached, she noticed something odd about the end hut. It looked as though it had been painted, of all colours – black, but as she got closer she could see it had been badly burnt although the actual structure appeared to be ok.

Libby was closing the blinds in the conservatory when she noticed the little red sports car had returned and was parked once again outside the old cottage just a little way further up the lane. There weren't any lights on inside and as Libby looked in the opposite direction, she noticed a tall, slim woman walking across the beach. She was sure it was the same woman who she had seen earlier in the afternoon go into the cottage and then hang around outside for a while before driving off again. All very mysterious. And here she was in the dark, walking across the beach, loaded with Saver-Shop carrier bags. Libby was transfixed.

"What are you nosing at Mum?" asked Jess, amused at the sight of her mother peering unashamedly out of the window into the darkness. "The neighbours might see you."

Libby ignored her daughter's comment. She knew none of her neighbours would be able to see her from their houses curving away down the lane.

"There's a strange woman down there on the beach. Heading towards the beach huts, I think."

Jess sidled over to her Mum and stood behind her, looking in the same direction to the far end of the beach where the huts were huddled together.

"She is. She's going in, to the one near the end. What do you make of that Jess? Weird eh?"

Libby turned to face her daughter but Jess had already disappeared from the room. When Libby looked back, the woman had disappeared into the hut and Libby, feeling like she was in the twilight zone, snatched the curtains shut in frustration.

Ella was relieved to finally reach the beach hut but it was dark and she struggled to unlock the padlock, fiddling with the tiny key she kept on her key ring. Once inside she lowered the carrier bags gently to the floor and felt for the light switch. A soft light cast a cosy warm glow over the inside of the hut highlighting the warm colourings of the soft furnishings. She pulled the rustic red and cream check curtains across the window to the front of the hut and threw the single bolt across the door, safe now in her own little sanctuary.

The winter evening air outside was bitter cold and damp and Ella was a little anxious to discover it wasn't much warmer inside. She had never been here at this time of year before. She remembered there was a small oil heater stored under the seats but noticed it was already set up as if it had been used recently. That was odd. Family and friends often used the beach hut but Ella couldn't recall that anyone had asked to use it lately. She looked about her, quite a few things were out of place and untidy but maybe, she thought, it just looked different because she hadn't been here for a while. She turned on the heater and had a quick tidy up, moving things back into place as she liked them. It was all done in a matter of minutes, making Ella smile at the thought of how easy it would be to keep her little cottage clean and tidy.

She unpacked her booty of goodies, feeling rather silly at the amount of stuff she'd bought. There was enough food to hold a birthday party for twenty children and they'd all be spoilt for choice. While the oven was heating with the lasagne inside, Ella made herself a cup of tea, snuggled under a crochet blanket and flicked through the magazines she'd bought. It was freezing and she was impatient for the hut to warm up.

Ella could hear the sea in the distance and apart from that there was just an eerie quiet, partly psychological due to her awareness of being alone in this hut, probably alone on the entire beach with just the vastness of the sea beyond.

In the silence she suddenly jumped when the shrill alarm sounded on the oven timer. The lasagne smelled delicious. Ella poured herself a glass of red wine and plonked the silver foil dish, piping hot, straight onto a plate – no ceremony tonight. The meal warmed her somewhat but the hut itself was still cold. Ella thought it best to settle herself in bed ready for another busy day tomorrow.

When they were first together, she and Jon had stayed at the hut almost every weekend. She couldn't wait to share it with him and for him to be a part of the place she loved so much. Later, he hardly had any weekends free and of course, she knew the reason for that now. They slept here in the seating area which could be pulled out into a bed but tonight she wanted it to be different to the previous times.

There was a loft area up in the rafters of the pitched roof which was boarded across to create another floor. Children of friends and family had slept here and made it into a comfy sleepover camp. And tonight, Ella decided it was going to be her camp. With the crochet blanket in one arm, she carefully climbed the small ladder which was more difficult than she thought. Once she was at the top, she calculated how many trips up and down she would have to make to fetch everything up she needed. Back on the ground again, she had a better idea. Ella gathered all the things together in a pile and then one by one, with careful aim, hurled them up to the loft to land softly on the bedding which consisted of a mattress on the floor and a collection of blankets and throws. A bag of crisps went up, a box of jam tarts, and after a couple of attempts, two magazines that, at first, came hurtling back down just missing her head.

Ella checked the door was properly locked and switched off the oil heater. Once again, she climbed the ladder and settled herself among the blankets. It was a bit of a mess up there but she resisted the urge to tidy it. She snuggled into the bedding and munched her way through a bag of cheese and onion crisps, looking through the home pages of the magazines, getting ideas for her cottage.

Ella smiled to herself, amused at her situation, tucked away in her beach hut all by herself, like a kid in a tree house. This wasn't how she imagined her first night to be but at least she was enjoying herself and that was a definite change for the better.

Ella had set the alarm on her mobile phone to go off at seven o'clock, early enough she thought to get herself ready and back to the cottage for when the removal men arrived. From her makeshift bed, Ella looked across to the wall opposite where a tiny window let in the daylight. She lay there and gazed at the beautiful clear blue skies welcoming in the day. From her warm snugly bed Ella could feel the air was cold in the hut but she needed to think about getting washed and dressed. A hot cup of tea would help to wake her up and keep her warm. It wasn't worth putting the oil heater on, it would take too long to get going. She sipped her tea warming both hands on the mug. A sausage roll and two jam tarts made for a quick breakfast and then she washed and dressed and began to tidy things away.

Ella climbed the ladder to bring her things down and saw properly, in the daylight, what a mess it was up there. She gathered some beer cans and wine bottles together, some chocolate wrappers and a discarded t-shirt and put them aside for the bin. She dragged the heavy quilt towards her and rolled it up neatly and then pulled the other various blankets and throws and folded them, mentally noting they could all do with a wash. The last one was held fast by the mattress and as she gave a strong tug, it freed itself together with a tatty plastic carrier bag. Ella shuddered to think what else might be lurking under the mattress. She shook the bag and was just about to put the empty cans in when she noticed there was already something inside. She peeked into the carrier bag and saw something wrapped in a black bin liner. Ella didn't like the look of it. She knelt down and emptied the carrier bag onto the floor, and with finger and thumb, shook out the contents of the bin bag. She watched with disbelief as piles of money; five pound, ten pound and twenty pound notes, possibly thousands of pounds, landed on the floor in front of her.

Chapter Six

Libby watched as the removal lorry reversed onto the drive of the old cottage. A man knocked at the door while the others prepared to unload. Now it all made sense, she thought; the woman who was here yesterday must have bought the place. Although it didn't explain why she had arrived a day early. Libby could see they were getting no reply and without hesitation, ran up the lane.

"Can I help you?"

"We're looking for Miss Peters."

"Yes, I think I know where I can find her. I'll be back in a few minutes."

"Cheers! We're not going anywhere."

Libby hurried off again, down the narrow steps and onto the beach and within a couple of minutes she was knocking at the door of the beach hut.

"Hello? Hello, good morning? Miss Peters?"

Ella opened the door, just a little and peeked around it. How did this woman know her name? The carrier bag of money was just behind her.

"Yes, I'm Miss Peters. Who are you please?"

Libby was a little taken aback. This nervous looking woman didn't look like the same woman who arrived yesterday in her bright red sports car, and who later marched across the beach on her own in the dark. Libby moved aside a little so she could see Ella better and so she could be better seen herself. And also to show that she was unarmed!

"I saw you, up at the old cottage yesterday."

Ella felt uneasy, what with thousands of pounds being stashed in her beach hut and now it seemed the locals were spying on her. Libby also felt rather uncomfortable. The woman had a very odd look on her face and still obviously didn't want to come out from behind the door. This wasn't a good start. She was beginning to feel like a nosey neighbour and this poor woman hadn't even moved in yet. She tried again.

"The old cottage, up on the lane?" Libby pointed back up the beach. "I live next door. It's been empty for a quite a while and then I saw you there yesterday. And then I saw you down here a bit later." Libby realised she was gabbling and probably not making any sense whatsoever. She stopped abruptly. Relaxed a little. Smiled. "A removal lorry has arrived. Would you like me to tell them you'll be along in a few minutes?"

Ella sighed with relief. "Yes, yes please, thank-you."

Libby turned and quickly walked back up the beach. Ella closed the door and leaned against it, smiling to herself. It was only her new next door neighbour she realised, feeling foolish. The woman must think her an idiot for cowering behind the door like that. She quickly gathered her things together, picked up the carrier bag full of money and looked around for somewhere to hide it but she couldn't think quick enough and so she stuffed it into another bag along with some groceries.

Ella half ran up the beach, passed the row of beach huts, noticing how some were bright and clean looking, having been recently painted. Others were faded with peeling paintwork and she knew her hut came into the latter category, not having been painted for a couple of years. She would have to get round to it this summer or she would be out of favour with the other hut owners.

She arrived at the cottage and the very welcome sight of the removal lorry and its occupants milling around on her driveway. She unlocked the door, keen for everyone to get started and they didn't need any prompting. The breakdown had put them behind and they needed to catch up otherwise they would find themselves working on into the night.

They began unloading immediately and pretty soon Ella felt as though she was in the way. The removal guys were speedy and efficient, helped by the fact that everything was clearly labelled, and whilst Ella tried to point them in the right direction for each piece of furniture and box they carried in, it was soon obvious they didn't really need her help. The removal company had put extra men on the job due to the breakdown and they were like ants, all over her house, busily, methodically and repeatedly moving things from one place to another. Wherever she stood, she still seemed to be in the way, constantly stepping aside or quickly darting backwards so as not to be barged out of the way by a bookcase or an armchair.

Ella wandered back outside, taking her bags with her, not wanting to leave the money lying around. She watched for a few minutes as they continued to unload her worldly goods and then strolled to the end of the drive. She turned and admired the exterior of her new home, squinting as the bright morning sunshine bounced off the whitewashed walls.

The next-door neighbour had disappeared and Ella looked along the lane in both directions wondering which way she lived. She decided to go for a quick stroll. There wasn't much she could do here for a while. Ella stopped a little further down the lane at the next house; a large house with a conservatory across the entire nearside. She stopped and looked up and instinctively felt that the woman lived here. And she was right. Libby had been sweeping leaves and suddenly appeared right in front of Ella.

"Oh hello. How's it going?" Libby had purposely kept out of the way. She would have liked to offer cups of coffee to her new neighbour but was even more keen to lose the prospective nosey neighbour tag.

"Fine thanks. I'm just letting them get on with it for a while."

Libby came closer and held out her garden gloved hand, still holding her broom in the other. "I'm Libby. Libby Pinkney. I hope you don't think I was being nosey, it's just that the place has been empty for some time and I couldn't help noticing your car there yesterday."

"No, it's fine, really. I'm Ella." They shook hands.

"Would you like to come in for a coffee? Just a quick one while your men are making a start."

Instinctively Ella was about to decline but she paused for just a second and was pleasantly surprised to hear herself answer as if it were someone else's voice. "Ok, yes I will, thanks." Ella followed Libby round the back into her house. Once in the large, family-sized kitchen, she was immediately struck by the warmth and homely comfort, and for a second wondered if she'd done the right thing by leaving her spacious home and down-sizing to the, by comparison, tiny cottage. Ella glanced around her, a mixture of school and sports bags lay on the floor. The warm air in the kitchen was infused with the smell of rich fresh coffee. It was such a cosy and welcoming home and it suddenly felt as though it would be a very long time before her cottage would be anywhere near as equally inviting.

Libby carried a tray and nodded at Ella to take a seat in one of the soft armchairs to the side of the kitchen. Ella sat down and placed her bags to the side of her, as Libby set down the tray.

"Help yourself. Excuse me; I'm just going to shout at the kids. They'll be late."

Ella helped herself to sugar and cream. The tray was laid with beautiful fine china. Everything in this house seemed perfect, Ella thought. The walls were covered in photos, mostly of the children winning awards or accomplishing some athletic feat worthy of making their parents proud. There was just one of Libby. She looked very young and glamorous in some sort of uniform. Ella couldn't help noticing there were no photos of their father.

"Todd, Jess! Get a move on, both of you."

Libby belted this out with surprising force. She sat down opposite Ella and smiled serenely.

"Normally, they're very good at getting themselves off to school. I don't know what they're up to this morning. A lot of whispering and plotting going on."

Ella pointed at the wall. "That's a nice photo of you."

Libby didn't need much prompting. "That was taken when I was an air hostess. I worked for British Airways for over ten years and became a senior hostess. And then of course when I got married and had the kids I had to give it up." Libby was obviously proud of her achievement and a little sad too, Ella thought, at the loss of her career. Ella didn't know what to say and so just smiled.

Libby's children bustled into the kitchen, grabbed their bags, mumbled "hello" to the stranger and "good-bye" to them both all in one sentence and were gone. Her daughter was slim with long blonde hair tied back in a sensible pony tail and her good-looking brother who was much taller had thick black hair flopping over his deep blue eyes. He looked older than his seventeen years.

"Mm, peace and quiet. I love this time of the morning when they've just got off to school and I get to have a nice cup of coffee before the day starts."

Ella smiled and drank some coffee.

"So, have you moved from far away?"

"Well, Gloucestershire - not too far. But I know it around here. I used to come here on family holidays when I was little." Ella sensed a barrage of questions and tried to stick to neutral ground. "You were saying the cottage had been empty for a while. That's surprising, it's such a lovely place."

"Mm, it is. It had quite a few viewings at first. It needs a bit of work doing, doesn't it? And I think that was putting people off. I'm glad it's going to be lived in again, it doesn't look nice for the village to have property sitting empty, getting all run down and ramshackle. Do you have plans for the place?"

"Well, nothing too major at first, there'll only be me living there."

Libby raised her eyebrows as she drank her coffee but Ella didn't elaborate. They drank in silence for a few moments and then Ella reached down for her bags.

"I hope you don't think I'm being rude dashing off but I feel I ought to get back."

"Oh no, of course, you get off. Perhaps I'll pop by later, see how you're doing. Would that be alright?"

"Yes, of course. Come over a bit later, hopefully I'll be more organised by then."

Back in the cottage, all the rooms were filling up fast. Several boxes had been stacked in the kitchen. Ella opened one to reveal carefully packed crockery. What she needed was to find the box with all the cleaning stuff so she could wash the cupboards before putting everything away.

A rattle at the back door made her jump and she looked up to see Libby knocking tentatively. As Ella moved towards the door, she was horrified to see Libby holding the carrier bag, the one that was stuffed full of money. What if she'd looked inside?

"Here, you left this behind." Libby was smiling and the look on her face reassured Ella although her hand was shaking as she took the bag. Libby came into the kitchen.

"Wow, the place looks so different without all the furniture. It was stuffed full before."

Ella casually threw the bag onto the worktop but missed. It fell to the floor with a thud revealing a package loosely wrapped in a black bin liner. Through a tear in the liner a few bundles of money spilled onto the kitchen floor.

Ella bent down and quickly bundled the money back in the bag. She stood to face Libby's bewildered expression but said nothing.

"Well, I'll leave you to it then," said Libby as she let herself out.

With some difficulty, Ella managed to light a small fire. She hadn't mastered the antiquated central heating system yet and resigned herself to being freezing cold on the first night in her new home. All the main furniture was in place although she was already planning to re-arrange most of it. She hadn't stopped all day yet there were countless unopened boxes in every room.

A hot bath had eased her aching body and a bowl of hot soup had warmed her insides, and now she was sitting on the floor to get the maximum benefit from the fire and finally relaxing with a glass of red wine. Ella gazed into the flames, the reality of the last couple of months creeping into her awareness.

It was quiet, she hadn't unpacked the television yet and the only sound was from the wind howling in from the sea, gusts buffeting the windows. Ella swirled the wine in the glass. This wasn't the celebratory feeling she was expecting after weeks of planning, sorting and packing. Tears stung her tired eyes but she sniffed them away. This was supposed to be a happy day.

A wave of loneliness washed over her but she put it down to tiredness. There suddenly seemed an awful lot to do and Ella felt momentarily overwhelmed with the responsibility of it all. She had been riding high on excitement over the past few weeks, the packing up of her old unhappy life and the anticipation of something new, a fresh start. But now she was actually here, the realisation that it would take quite some time to put her new life in place was very daunting.

The carrier bag containing the money was close by her on the floor, and she sighed at the burden of having to decide what to do with it. A little earlier she had counted the money and was relieved to discover it wasn't anywhere near the tens of thousands of pounds she had first imagined. It was just over three and a half thousand pounds but still, she didn't have a clue what she should do with it.

Ella sat there for a while until her limbs went numb on the cold thinly carpeted floor. She pulled the old fireguard across what was left of the fire and went upstairs feeling the decrease in temperature with each stair she climbed and drafts from almost every direction on the small landing. Perhaps she had under-estimated the amount of repair work to be done, maybe the windows needed replacing as well as the heating.

In the bedroom, Ella's heart sank as she realised she hadn't made up the bed. At least she had managed to throw some linen and the duvet into a pile on top. She threw a sheet across the bed without bothering to tuck it in, grabbed a pillow and pulled the duvet and an assortment of blankets roughly across her, not really expecting to get a wink of sleep. But despite the cold and the makeshift conditions, she fell into a deep sleep within seconds.

Chapter Seven

"Mum! The neighbours are gonna start talking about you if you don't stop nosing!"

Libby turned from the window and smiled at her daughter but judging from the expression on her face, she wasn't sure if her comment was intended as a joke.

"I'm only looking out of the window at the lovely view. That's what lovely views are for – looking at." A sideways glance enabled Libby to see Jess's face had softened just a little.

"And the fact that our new neighbour just happens to be walking across the beach, is just a coincidence." Libby smiled again as Jess joined her at the window.

"Where's she going?" asked Jess.

"Looks like she's on her way to her beach hut again. She spent the night in there, you know?"

"Are you and her gonna be friends?"

"Well, yes, she seems nice enough. Why?"

Libby turned to see her teenage daughter give the typical non-committal shrug before leaving the room without saying a word. Libby sighed, she was about to ask what had been going on that morning. Someone was up and about unusually early for a Saturday and whoever had gone out hadn't taken the dog for a walk because she remembered him barking. Libby went into the kitchen to load the dishwasher. She had a grim feeling this was going to be a long weekend.

Ella had spent the last few days arranging and rearranging furniture and was just beginning to feel satisfied with her efforts. This morning she felt the need to get out of the house. Despite the grey skies she decided to go for a walk along the beach and call in at the hut. She thought she might have left some perishable food behind and didn't like the idea of it rotting and stinking the place out.

She still hadn't decided what to do with the money she'd found. She kept putting it in a different hiding place, just the sight of it made her feel uneasy.

As soon as she was out on the beach Ella realised she had misjudged the weather. The wind was whipping around her, numbing her ears and nose. She wished she'd wrapped up better and decided to head straight for the beach hut to shelter for a few moments. And she was sure there was a weatherproof jacket there.

Seeing the row of huts in the distance she couldn't help but smile at how charming they looked. She loved the way they were all the same but slightly different and that inside each hut was a secret little world as individual as its owner. Ella came alongside the huts hoping they would act as a wind-break but instead the wind whistled in between them. She could hear something banging above the noise of the wind, and turned to see it was the door to her hut swinging open and shut. At first she assumed she hadn't locked it properly in her hurry to meet with the removal lorry earlier in the week, but as she walked up the steps and onto the deck, she could see the little padlock on the floor and that it had been broken open.

Ella grabbed the door and held it tight against the wind to stop it banging, listening cautiously in the doorway, all of a sudden very aware of her solitariness tucked away by the huts on the beach. She could feel and hear her heart thudding as she stepped silently inside. One quick sweep of a look confirmed with relief there was no-one inside – unless, of course, they were up in the loft maybe looking for their money.

There was no way Ella was brave enough to climb the ladder only to come face to face with an angry somebody wondering where their three thousand pound stash was. She stared, eyes fixed on the loft. She knew she hadn't made a sound but if there was someone up there, they might be curious as to why the door had suddenly stopped banging. She continued to stare half expecting a head to peek out. But nothing. Carefully, and as quietly as possible, she closed the door. In one swift movement she grabbed the small square coffee table with one hand and dragged it towards her. She leaped up on it, scouring the loft and confirming immediately there was no-one up there. Although someone obviously had been there at some point; the bedclothes Ella had neatly folded were tossed all over the place and the mattress itself had been moved and left over on the far side of the loft floor.

Ella stepped down from the table and looked about her. It didn't look like anything had been taken – not that there was much to take. In fact, it didn't look like anything else had even been touched. Whoever had broken in was obviously only after one thing.

Ella snatched a carrier bag from a drawer, fear and adrenalin coming out in temper. She slammed the drawer shut. Who had done this to her? She threw the opened packets of cooked meat and cheese inside. The idea of speaking to Jon immediately came to her mind as it still did whenever one of life's little challenges reared its ugly head. There was no-one here to speak to and everything felt more acute when dealing with it on her own. She thought about stopping by at Libby's house but she hadn't seen her since the day she moved in when Libby brought the bag back with all the money in it.

She plonked the carrier bag by the door, grabbed the oilskin jacket that was hanging up and put it on. The wind wasn't letting up and it had started to rain too but she didn't want to hang around the hut any longer than she had to.

Ella knelt down and rummaged in the cupboard under the worktop and found a small piece of rope to secure the door. As she stood she saw a small silver stud earring in the shape of a skull – not very pretty thought Ella, putting it into her pocket, wondering who of her friends or family might have lost it. Outside she tied the rope through the metal loop where the padlock had been, reassuring herself it would be ok to leave the hut without being properly locked and immediately grimaced at the irony of that thought.

Ella pulled up her jacket hood, holding it tight to protect her face from the wind and rain and ran back up the beach, up the steps and onto the lane. She slowed down as she reached her own cottage and then carried on passed it, towards Libby's house. She knocked tentatively on the front door debating whether to turn and go back home and then Libby appeared immediately opening the door wide beckoning her inside.

"My god, what's happened to you? Come in quick, before you drown."

Ella stepped inside the porch as Libby helped her off with her jacket. She slipped her Wellingtons off and left them on the mat and followed Libby through the conservatory to the kitchen. After a relatively cold week in the cottage, still struggling to get the heating working properly, Ella relished the luxuriant warmth of Libby's home; three hundred and sixty degree heat that seemed to swathe her entire body.

Ella took her place again in one of the armchairs. Libby seemed completely unruffled by her sudden appearance.

"Tea or coffee?"

"Oh, tea please."

"Are you ok? Is everything alright at the cottage? I thought I'd leave you to it for a while."

"Not really, no. I'd like to talk to you about something. I hope you don't mind me just turning up like this. I went for a walk along the beach huts."

"Funny day for a walk." Libby smiled warmly carrying a tray of hot drinks. "It's horrible out there."

"Yes it is. I've been busy in the cottage and just felt the need to get out for a while."

"How's everything coming along? Bet you feel like you'll never be organised don't you?"

"Mm." Ella took a sip of tea.

"So, what's up?"

"Well," Ella put down her cup. "My beach hut's been broken into."

"What? That's terrible. It really is. Has anything been taken or damaged? What gets into these people's minds?"

"No, but I do think they were looking for something."

At that moment Jess and Todd came running noisily down the stairs, shouting at each other. Libby was straight out of her chair as the two teenagers bundled into the kitchen.

"What is up with you two lately? That's enough!"

Todd put his head in the fridge. "Tell her to leave it out then. She's a pain."

Jess was grinning. "He's sulking 'cos he lost his earring."

"No I'm not." Todd left the kitchen without any food and slumped himself in front of the television. Jess was laughing.

"I think his girlfriend bought it for him. A stupid skull thing."

"Sounds charming," said Libby. "And I don't think he's allowed to wear an earring to school."

"He's not. He takes it off in the morning and puts it on again after school. It's probably still in his pocket." Jess sloped off out of the kitchen, leaving Ella and Libby alone again.

Actually, it's in my pocket, thought Ella, feeling for the metal stud through the fabric of her jeans.

Libby sat down heavily and rolled her eyes, shaking her head. "Sorry about that. Now, what were you saying? Your poor hut. Oh, gosh, yes, you thought they were looking for something? Why do you think that?"

"Well, I'm not really sure. A few things were turned about."

"Oh that's horrible. I bet it makes you feel violated – people going through your personal things."

"Well, no, it isn't that bad – really. They probably meant no harm. I've likely got it wrong. Probably just kids messing around."

"I don't know that I would be so gracious if it was my lovely beach hut they'd ransacked."

They sipped their tea in thoughtful silence.

"You ought to report it, you know. To the police."

"No it's ok, there's nothing taken and no damage done. I'll make sure I secure it up properly from now on."

Libby sighed wearily. "It makes me sad. I know this is a cliché but the place isn't what it used to be. Now it seems everyone has got an intruder alarm, fancy security lighting, panic buttons, the lot. Kids often get the blame for any trouble – they get bored, don't know what to do with themselves."

"They shouldn't be bored here, right on the seafront, with all the gorgeous beaches and loads to do."

Libby smiled. "You never appreciate what's on your doorstep, do you?"

"No, maybe you're right."

"Oh and talking of getting bored like my two this morning. I want to say, if you ever need any little odd jobs doing – keep my Todd in mind. I'm trying to teach him the work ethic, and that money doesn't grow on trees. Mind you, he never seems to want for money. I think his father keeps him supplied but doesn't tell me. So, anyway, if you need any help in the cottage or the garden or with your beach hut, just give me a nod ok?"

"Ok, thanks, I'll bear it in mind." She stood to leave, feeling hot and tingly with anxious tension.

"Oh, are you off? I was hoping we could sit and chat all morning. It's still awful out there. Looks like the rain is here to stay."

Ella was more than eager to leave. She was already in the porch pulling on a welly but in her desperate hurry all she could do was hop around on the spot like someone in a comedy sketch. After a deep breath and a concerted effort to calm herself, she was ready to leave.

"It's nice to see you. Anytime you fancy, just pop over for a coffee."

Libby's cordial invitation seemed touchingly genuine to Ella, making the secret she'd just discovered all the more unwelcome and difficult to conceal. And she was not pleased about it.

Chapter Eight

Libby had invited Francine over for coffee and had been fussing all morning, tweaking things in place, checking Mrs O'Brien had followed her instructions to the letter when she came in yesterday for an extra day of cleaning. Libby wanted everything to be just perfect. This was a definite step in the right direction, becoming good friends with Francine Lawrence.

She had changed into her most expensive cream cashmere sweater and wore it with camel coloured trousers – trying to emulate the stylish neutral colour scheme that Francine did so well. She was tempted to go with her favourite colours of navy and cream, perhaps with a red scarf. These reminded her of her air hostess days and the uniform which made her feel smart and efficient.

Libby paced between rooms trying to decide where was most impressive, her beautiful bespoke kitchen designed to her very exacting specifications or the glamorous conservatory which was the envy of everyone who visited. In the end she decided on the lounge, a slightly more formal setting but with good views of the landscaped garden. She had considered baking some pastries for the occasion but had decided in the end to buy in and had gone to Juliette's bakery. They sold exquisite little French style pastries and cakes which were outrageously expensive but worth it for their impressiveness, Libby thought, trying to justify her decision.

It was just a few minutes after the hour and Libby hoped Francine hadn't forgotten her. She puffed and re-puffed cushions and once again stood in the conservatory checking the lane for Francine's car. And there it was, just pulling up alongside the kerb.

Libby opened the front door and noted immediately the flattering fit of Francine's jeans and the casual but incredibly stylish red polo neck and colourful silk scarf tied neatly at the neck.

"Hello, am I early? I couldn't remember the time we said."

"No, it's fine, really. Come on in."

Libby showed Francine through to the lounge and went back to the kitchen to make the coffee, finally presenting it on an ornate silver tray with a two tier cake stand stacked with the delicate pastries. It all looked very classy. Francine was smiling and Libby suddenly wasn't sure she hadn't gone a little over the top.

"Oh Libby, this looks divine. Thank you. Did you make all these yourself? I've heard you're quite a whiz on the catering side of things."

Libby felt a little flustered as well as flattered and now wished desperately that she had made the effort to do some baking after all.

"No, I didn't make these but I do enjoy cooking. These are from Juliette's, it's a little French style bakery in Bridge Street, do you know it?"

"Yes I do, it's my favourite – I go there all the time."

Francine took a pretty tea plate and helped herself to a dainty pastry. She was used to women being nervous in her company and over-doing the welcome and charm but she quite liked Libby. She thought she could be a useful friend to have.

"I'm giving some thought to this year's mid-summer party, it's all change this year. Remember that terrible storm last winter? And The Grange got hit by lightening? Well, apparently some twit from the health and safety department has deemed it unsafe for public events. Hm, it's probably been like that for years and we've all been risking our lives all in the name of some charity fund. Anyway, I've been asked to step in so I've said it can be held at our place but not in the house, definitely not in the house. They can put a marquee on the lawn – I don't mind as long as it's all put right afterwards."

"That sounds nice," said Libby.

"It'll be a lot of hard work I expect. You don't fancy helping out do you? Perhaps help with organising the catering or something? Or anything actually. You realise who your true friends are, when there's real work to be done." Francine laughed.

"I'd love to help Francine, really I would," said Libby with great enthusiasm. She felt truly honoured to be asked but managed to refrain from actually saying so.

"That's great – really kind of you. It's not until August so we've got plenty of time but we'll need to get together now and then if that's ok with you? Next time you come to me for coffee and we can go through the preliminaries."

"Ok, that sounds lovely."

Francine was delighted at how easy it had been to get Libby on board. Buoyed up with satisfaction she asked, "How do you fancy a weekend in Bath? A group of us are off at the weekend, gorgeous hotel, plenty of shopping, should be fun, what do you say?"

Libby could have jumped for joy. "Sounds fantastic, I'd love to come. And I'll think up some ideas for the mid-summer party."

The idea of a summer party right here in the middle of the village was incredibly exciting. In previous years it had been held at The Grange which was a few miles out of the village and had always been a rather half-hearted effort. All the villagers were invited but it was never a great turn out.

This year it would be perfect. If Francine and Roger were hosting it, everyone would go. Libby would have the chance to shine in front of everyone she knew and really impress Francine.

Francine stood up and walked over to the French windows, looking out into the garden.

"I notice you have a new neighbour. Someone's finally bought the old cottage?"

"Yes, a woman on her own, Ella."

"What's she like?"

"She's nice, yes, very nice."

"Invite her along next week too. She might be willing to pitch in – the more the merrier, as they say."

Libby offered Francine more coffee and took the tray back to the kitchen. Without knowing why exactly, she knew for sure she wouldn't be inviting Ella to Bath.

Chapter Nine

It had been dark all afternoon and Ella found it depressing. The days were getting longer signifying the arrival of spring but it was still very cold. Black storm clouds had gathered and were crowding the sky and now they hovered low over the beach. The wind was getting stronger and the willow tree was straining as it was forced to bend, its heavy branches bouncing rhythmically. Just beyond the willow tree, the tops of the tall conifers flipped about frantically.

Ella peered through the window, out to where the sea should be but what looked like a black expanse of nothing. Rain began thrashing against the windows and Ella closed the curtains and stood in front of the fire. She picked up a birthday card from the mantelpiece and read inside, 'Happy Birthday dear Ella, love from Aunty Barbara'. Aunty Barbara was in fact her great-aunt and had lived in Australia for the last thirty years. Ella had vague memories of her from her childhood but they hadn't seen each other in all that time or even spoken on the telephone but every year Ella got a birthday card. Like this one, it usually arrived weeks too early. She thought her elderly aunt probably didn't trust in modern technology and the ability to transport mail to the other side of the world in just a few days.

Aunt Barbara had sent a parcel too but it had been delivered next door as it was too large for her letterbox - so the card informed her that had a tick in the appropriate box. She replaced the birthday card on the mantelpiece and tried to settle on the sofa.

Ella hadn't seen Libby for a couple of weeks. She hadn't been avoiding her exactly but acknowledged she was keeping a low profile. She had put off calling next door for the parcel all day and when she finally knocked in the early evening, the house was in complete darkness except for the security light that flicked on as soon as she went up the drive. There was obviously no-one home and Ella didn't hang around, relieved she still didn't have to face Libby yet.

She was in a real quandary over the whole money-in-the-hut thing. Finding the skull earring and Todd losing a skull earring, he'd obviously broken into the beach hut either on his own or with his mates, looking for the money. She didn't want to even think about what he might be up to. And the whole question of whether or not she should tell Libby was driving her half mad.

There seemed to be no easy resolution to this whole episode. And even to do nothing was not to do the right thing. Ella found herself increasingly annoyed with Todd for putting her in this position and she began to think she had no option but to confront him direct. That was it – she had decided. She would speak to Todd first, give him an opportunity to defend himself and then take things from there.

An extreme gush of wind pounded at the windows sending a bracing draught across the room as Ella slipped from the sofa, dropped to the floor and walked on her knees across the thin shabby carpet onto the new cream rug she'd recently bought and sat cross-legged as close to the fire as she dared. The windows rattled in their casings. Ella had decided they would all have to be replaced by next winter, so great were the draughts in every nook and cranny of the cottage.

She felt better now. Having found a halfway solution to the problem she could now file it away in her mind and leave it there for a while until she was ready to tackle the next step which was to create an opportunity to talk to Todd.

Ella reached up to the mantelpiece and carefully retrieved a glass of red wine she'd left there earlier. She was surprised and disappointed to feel the glass was still cold. She placed it on the hearth, so it could be warmed by the fire, reached up and once again lifted the birthday card from the mantelpiece. On the front was a cartoon picture of an alarm clock which was surrounded by various cartoon animals. The heading read 'It's Time....' and inside the card, predictably, 'To Wish You a Happy Birthday'. Ella smiled at what she saw as the irony of it. Time was indeed ticking by – she would be thirty-seven in just a few weeks. And this wasn't how she imagined she would be spending birthdays in her thirties; alone, single, childless with precious time running out not leaving her much opportunity to be able to do anything to change it.

A particularly chilly draught whistled around Ella's back making her shudder as she pulled her jumper down over the gap of her jeans. She fidgeted a little and changed her position on the rug, turning to face the room slightly so her back could be warmed by the fire.

She cast her eyes over the room. It didn't look homely to her. The threadbare tatty carpet and dingy wallpaper did nothing to compliment her nice furniture which still looked too crowded in this small room no matter how much she re-arranged it. A nauseous wave of loneliness washed over her as she stared into the flames of the fire blaming their brightness for the stinging tears which were beginning to form.

A sharp sound at the window caused her to snatch her gaze from the fire. It was probably just a loose twig caught in the wind, she thought. She hoped. Just a little way along the lane there, was Libby's house. She realised now, the comfort she got from knowing she had someone friendly so close by and she regretted being so distant over the last couple of weeks. Perhaps if she had made more effort, Libby might have explained where she was off to this weekend and when she would be back whereas the fact that Libby's house was empty tonight only added to her loneliness.

Chapter Ten

Ella had spent yet another morning re-arranging furniture in the kitchen diner. She was physically exhausted and now thoroughly fed-up too, as she came to the conclusion that it all looked better before. She needed a strong coffee and put the kettle on trying not to think about the chocolate in the fridge. While she waited for the kettle to boil, she looked around at the state of the kitchen. The furniture was too big for the scale of the room and it looked clumsy and cluttered. Ella took her mug of coffee and the chocolate and stepped out into the garden, closing the door firmly on the chaos inside.

The previous owner had obviously been much keener on gardening than interior decorating judging by the neat and tidy arrangement of flower beds. Ella was determined to keep on top of it as spring came along. She was looking forward to the changing seasons and to discovering what would appear in the garden throughout the year; lots of daffodils soon she thought, looking at the mass of green shoots peeking through the soil

Ella walked to the end of the garden and stood, marvelling at the glorious view of the bay below. She stood still in the brilliant sunshine, pleasantly surprised to discover how warm it was and tilted her head back, closed her eyes and basked in what she imagined to be rejuvenating energies. She walked back up the garden towards the house, in its shadow and out of the sun now, perching on the edge of a garden bench which was still damp from the overnight dew. She surveyed the garden and thought it amusing, the way it seemed to match the cottage with its different levels up and down.

Ella thought she glimpsed the red of Libby's coat through the gate, and immediately went over to investigate. Libby was already letting herself in.

"Hi Ella. How are you?"

"Hi Libby, it's really lovely to see you."

"How's the cottage coming along?"

"I'm having a bit of a nightmare actually. Re-arranging furniture. I think I preferred it as it was - about three hours ago!"

"You're probably trying to do too much too soon."

"I'd like to get it looking nice though. And feel settled."

They walked into the kitchen together, Libby was holding a small package wrapped in brown paper. "Oh here, this is for you, it arrived at mine last Friday. I meant to bring it over before I went away for the weekend but completely forgot – I'm so sorry."

"It's ok, really, it's just a birthday present although it's not for weeks yet."

"Oh? Really? You have a birthday coming up? Well, we must do something about that."

"I don't think I want to celebrate birthdays anymore, it just means you're getting older."

Libby was already thinking ahead. This was an opportunity not to be missed. "We'll think of something nice to do, nothing too over the top, don't you worry." Libby looked around the kitchen, inspecting and nodding in approval.

"Your furniture looks fine. You haven't been here that long, give yourself some time. And things will fall into place - naturally."

"You make it sound so easy. And your house is really gorgeous. How long have you lived there?"

"Since before the kids were born - getting on for twenty years actually."

Ella groaned at the prospect of it taking even half that time to get her home organised.

"Ok, I'm off, just wanted to pop your parcel over. I'll leave you to move all your furniture back as it was."

They both laughed.

"Do you fancy lunch one day next week?" Libby asked.

"Yes, I do. That would be lovely."

"Good. Let's say Thursday at 1:00pm –looking forward to it."

"Me too."

Ella settled for a simple grey jersey dress which emphasised her tall, slim figure, casual and not too dressy. She arranged her hair in a loose knot and looked in the mirror, not convinced she'd achieved the look she was after which she concluded might be due to the fact that she wasn't entirely sure what look she was after. Ella went downstairs, sort of happy with herself, just as Libby's car pulled up outside. Ella waved to signal she was ready and on her way out.

They chatted easily on the drive to the restaurant about nothing in particular.

Libby parked in the car park at the rear of the Chez André Restaurant, a French restaurant she'd been to many times. The warmth and smell of delicious good food was very welcoming and Ella smiled to herself as she realised how much she was enjoying herself.

"Table for two in the name of Pinkney," said Libby.

They were shown to their table, which was a comfortable distance from a small open fire. The restaurant was quiet this lunch time with just a small group of women who were obviously celebrating something judging by the assortment of cards and presents littering their table, and an elderly couple who looked very comfortable as if maybe they came here every Thursday at the same time at the same table.

Libby and Ella sat down opposite each other. One second of awkward silence had them picking up their menus and studying them intently. In another second the awkwardness was gone and they debated whether to have a light lunch or a full blown three course meal. They agreed to compromise with a main meal and dessert.

"I can recommend, if you'd like. I come here whenever I can. I love it. Actually, I was in Paris a few months ago. You ever been?"

Ella had been to Paris. Just the once. Jon had arranged the weekend trip, and had proposed to her as they walked along the banks of the Seine, arm in arm, on a warm summer evening. She hadn't seen it coming but it had been a fantastic surprise, unlike the surprise she felt now. She had been totally unprepared for the question and was suddenly speechless. She could feel her eyes beginning to fill with tears and she knew her cheeks were red.

"Ella, are you ok?"

"It's just my contacts playing up. I'll be back in a sec." Ella dashed out to the ladies' toilet. She locked herself in a cubicle, feeling totally stupid and strangely disappointed in herself at how such an innocent reference could cause her to crumble, again.

After just a couple of minutes, Ella felt composed enough to go back to the table. As she walked through the restaurant, she saw Libby standing chatting with a man. His hand was placed gently on her waist – a relaxed and yet intimate gesture. Perhaps this was the elusive husband. As she got closer she was surprised to notice the man was quite a bit older than Libby – maybe in his early sixties. He was tall and broad, an overall good stature. His thick hair was almost completely white with just a few areas of dark grey showing through. He was lightly tanned and he smiled warmly at her as she approached. Most striking of all were his warm brown eyes which caused her to look away as soon as they connected with hers and then feeling like a silly schoolgirl she tried to compose herself even though she knew her cheeks were glowing. He smiled gently as though he could sense her discomfort. Perhaps he had this effect on all the women he met, thought Ella. Well, Libby was a lucky lady – no wonder she had a permanent smile. Ella held out her hand.

"You must be Mr Pinkney?"

"That's right. And you are?"

"Ella Peters. I'm your new neighbour, I've just moved into the old cottage, just up the lane from you."

He smiled down at Libby with his eyebrows raised.

Libby explained. "Ella, this is Andrew. He's not my husband, he's my father-in-law. Well, my ex-father-in-law." They looked at each other and laughed. "Oh, well, you know what I mean."

Ella did, just about. There was a lot of information in that one sentence.

"Ok, I'll leave you ladies to it. Very nice to meet you Ella."

Libby and Ella sat back down.

"Sorry about that. I shouldn't have assumed."

"Oh don't worry, it's fine."

"He seems really nice."

"Andrew – he's lovely. A very good friend."

Ella nodded, curious but cautious not to step into unwelcome territory but Libby continued.

"People often assume we're a couple." Libby smiled as she twiddled the stem of her glass between her fingers. "Andrew's very popular around here."

Ella looked past Libby towards the entrance where a group of people were just arriving. Andrew was chatting and smiling warmly as if he had all the time in the world. Libby noticed the direction of Ella's gaze and turned in her seat just as Andrew finally managed to leave the restaurant.

"I think it's nice that you're still close." Ella was thinking of her own relationship with Colette and what a great friend and comfort she had been.

"Yes, we are, very close." She had the secret smile again and for a fleeting moment Ella couldn't help wondering if there was a little something more than just friendship between Libby and Andrew.

But Libby changed the direction of conversation and Ella was happy just to sit and listen to this attractive, smiling woman.

"Me and my husband, David, we divorced five years ago. Libby took a sip of her wine, clasped her hands together on the table and looked squarely at Ella. "We realised we weren't really a couple anymore." Libby smiled and gave a little laugh. "We'd separated before we separated, if you know what I mean. We had our own friends and our own lives and I think when it got to the point where we were doing things with the kids on our own, you know, taking them out separately – well, we had to admit we weren't a proper family anymore. It seemed the right thing to just go our own ways."

Libby took another sip of wine and then another. "Mm, this is lovely – can't beat a good Chilean."

Ella was completely absorbed by Libby's story. She picked up her glass and took several large gulps wondering how on earth she could tone down the dramas of her own marriage breakdown. Her new friend seemed to reside in a warm and colourful Disney cartoon version of life. How could Ella explain hers was more like A Tale of the Unexpected?

"Do your children get to see much of their father?"

"They go to see him every other weekend – he only lives across town, so it all works very well."

"It certainly seems to."

"Like I said, it seemed the right thing to do – for everyone. And we get on fine now – well, mostly." Libby grinned, shrugged her shoulders and took another sip of wine, her cheeks becoming quite rosy. Ella gazed at Libby sitting opposite. She was a perfect picture of beauty, health and happiness. She could almost see a Hollywood style soft focus mist envelope her outline.

"Ok, you're giving me a weird look now. What have I said? That I get on with my ex-husband?"

Ella realised she'd been staring. "Sorry Libby. Yes, it does seem, rather, well unusual."

"Well, when you have kids, it's different." Ella felt the sting of her innocent comment. "You have to be able to communicate. They're always going to be there between you. Actually, I don't see him often, just sometimes when he drops the kids off. But we do talk on the phone quite a lot. I suppose I am quite lucky, really."

Ella couldn't stop herself from frowning as she thought about the enormity of that under-statement. Seeing Ella's puzzled face, Libby leaned forward slightly and placed her hand on Ella's arm. "You're divorced too, are you?"

"Yes, that's right." Ella braced herself for the inevitable barrage of questions. But instead Libby snatched her hand back and sat upright as the waiter arrived with their food.

"Ooh, that looks good," said Libby examining her plate of seafood medley; a fresh selection of fish and shellfish in a rich creamy sauce. "And yours looks a good choice too." Libby took another sip of wine and tucked in. Ella felt momentarily relieved as she started on her salmon in champagne sauce but after they had eaten in silence for a few minutes, she began to feel dejected. She wanted to resume the conversation. Suddenly she wanted Libby to know about her past, about Jon and his silly young wife, and of the heartbreak that had nearly destroyed her when she found out they were to have a baby. She just wanted Libby to know and understand what she'd been through. It would be a release to finally unload this burden, to lower the barrier a little between her and the world and stop pretending to everyone that everything was ok.

The waiter appeared at their table. "Is everything ok ladies?" Libby asked for a new pepper mill as theirs had run out. The waiter apologised profusely, almost bowing as he shuffled away. The moment for deep and meaningful conversation had passed.

They enjoyed the rest of their meal and then for dessert did what the menu suggested which was to share a platter of mixed chocolate indulgence. The glutinous assortment of chocolate and more wine soon had them chatting again. Libby poured the last of the wine into Ella's glass.

"Here, you finish this, I've got to drive back although I could quite easily order another bottle and stay here all afternoon."

Ella was pleased Libby was enjoying herself and was pleased to acknowledge she was too. "We'll have to do it again – soon."

Libby screwed up her nose; she didn't want the fun to end just yet. "I've got a better idea, let's go back to mine. I've got more bottles in the fridge and the kids are off to a rugby match after school so we don't have to be grown up and sensible for hours. What do you say?"

Ella grinned, it sounded like a good idea. Libby called for the bill and insisted on paying, and then she drove the short journey back, pointing out the close proximity of Andrew's house on the way.

Once indoors, Libby opened another bottle of wine and served it in fine crystal glasses. They each sat on a huge soft sofa on either side of a large square coffee table. The room was warm and cosy albeit on a grand scale. Ella felt comfortable and relaxed and slipped off her shoes, tucking her legs underneath her. They stayed there until early evening, drinking and chatting and laughing out loud.

"Now, what shall we do about your birthday party?" asked Libby.

"I don't really want a party Libby, honestly, it's not my kind of thing."

"Ok, ok, we won't have a party, just a few people over, some of the other neighbours and Andrew – he'll come along."

At that moment Andrew walked into the lounge, making both women jump.

"What will I come along to?"

"Andrew, you frightened the life out of me." Libby jumped up and was instantly fetching another wine glass for him.

"I did knock – you two were making so much noise, anyone could have come in. Told you before Libby to keep the door locked." Andrew was serious but he had a caring twinkle in his eye.

Libby handed Andrew his glass, beaming appreciatively at his kind concern. "Come and sit down."

Libby returned to her seat and Andrew settled himself on the other sofa.

"Hello Ella," he said.

"Hello – ," it seemed too familiar to use his name and once again Ella felt self-conscious in the company of this elderly gentleman. She straightened her legs off the sofa and sat up a little straighter, very aware of Andrew's presence close to her.

"We were just discussing what to do for Ella's birthday in a few weeks."

Ella still had reservations about the whole idea. Part of her just wanted the day to slip by without any ceremony.

"Libby, I'm still not sure about all this. My cottage is a long way off being fit for guests. They'd freeze for one thing."

"Oh, don't be silly – I'll hold the party here. Lay on a bit of food, now don't worry, nothing formal, just friends and family for some drinks and nibbles."

Ella was quite over-whelmed at Libby's kindness and decided in that moment to make an effort to get into the party spirit. It now seemed ungracious not to accept.

A loud rattle followed by vigorous banging at the back door had them all jumping in their seats this time, although Libby quickly realised what had happened. She went through to the kitchen, unlocked the door, and let in two very annoyed teenagers.

"Mum, you locked us out!" said Jess, shivering dramatically. "It's flippin' cold out there," she said, as if to suggest that the few extra seconds outside might be life threatening.

"Andrew's here, he probably locked it, to protect me from the horrors out there in the night." Libby glared at her over-reacting children, who were already fishing in the fridge.

"Come through and say hello in a minute."

Libby returned to the lounge. Ella was staring into her glass, tuning into the voices of Libby's children in the kitchen. She looked across at Libby wondering how let down and disappointed she would be to discover what her son had been up to. Fuelled by her anger at being caught up into this situation, together with a little alcohol-induced bravado, she was prompted to do something about it.

"Libby, I've been thinking; about my beach hut. I've been neglecting it for years and it's looking really tatty, needs a bit of shooshing up."

"I love your beach hut," Libby interrupted. "It's my favourite one out of the whole lot of them. I've had my eye on buying it for years. Will you sell it to me?" Libby laughed while Ella smiled and shook her head.

"No, I don't blame you, I wouldn't sell it either, if it were mine."

"Libby, you remember you said Todd maybe interested in a bit of work in the holidays? Well, Easter's not far off and I wondered if he'd be interested in doing some painting for me, definitely the outside of the hut and maybe the inside too – smarten the whole place up."

"I'm sure he'll be fine with that. In fact, I'll make sure he is."

"That's great then." Ella stood, it had been a lovely day but she was ready to go home now and then Jess and Todd entered the room.

"Todd, Ella has got some work for you over Easter, painting her lovely beach hut, that's ok with you, isn't it?"

Todd looked warily at Ella, sandwich in hand, halfway to his mouth. He swallowed hard before speaking. "Not sure, I might have plans."

Jess didn't miss an opportunity to interject. "Plans? Yeah, like you've got such a busy schedule."

"Jess, shh," reprimanded Libby.

Ella moved towards the door and closer to Todd. They were face to face, just a foot apart, and she had a sudden rush of courage from somewhere, and in a lowered voice with just a hint of warning said, "I pay well. In cash. I have lots of cash."

Todd held her eye contact and she stared back. He took a big bite of his sandwich and with a full mouth mumbled something which sounded like, "Ok, I'll do it."

Chapter Eleven

Early April, a week into the Easter holidays and it had rained every day so far. Ella was psyched up for her confrontation with Todd and she was annoyed at the thought that she wouldn't have her chance to get to the bottom of all this.

At last the rain petered out, leaving fresh blue skies dotted with fluffy clouds which were being blown along by a stiff breeze. The forecast for tomorrow was good and a quick telephone call to Libby confirmed Todd would meet Ella at the hut in the morning at nine-thirty.

Ella had bought the paint and brushes and stored them in the hut ready. There were no local authority regulations regarding colour but the hut owners had fallen in with an unspoken agreement and adopted a traditional blue and white colour scheme. As she walked across the beach she could see Todd already there waiting. He saw her coming towards him and shuffled about self-consciously, looking down at his feet as he lightly kicked the sand.

"Morning Todd. How are you?"

"Ok," he mumbled, still avoiding her gaze.

"Sorry to get you up so early. Don't worry, I'll make it worth your while." Ella cringed at what she'd just said; it was loaded with innuendo and not what she meant at all. She walked up the steps and unlocked the large, brand new padlock, wondering if Todd had observed this detail. She walked inside and turned to see Todd slowly climbing the steps with typical teenage reluctance. Ella found it both amusing and irritating.

"Ok, I think I've got everything you might need. This is all the stuff for the outside. Don't worry about that lot over there, that's for the inside if there's time." Ella wasn't sure how long Todd would continue to work for her, especially once she'd had her say.

They stood in silence for a few seconds. Ella realised she wasn't ready at that moment to ask Todd about the break-in at the hut. She didn't know how to start the conversation and right now, it didn't seem right.

"Are you ok if I leave you to it then?" Todd nodded, non-committal. Ella suddenly realised she had no idea if Todd had any previous painting experience or whether he would even know where to start. She would expect him to remove all the old flaking paint and give the wood a light rub down before painting it again. She walked back up the beach fighting the temptation to look back to see if he was ok. She couldn't help wondering, with some trepidation, what exactly she would find when she did return. Just as she got to the stone steps taking her back up to the lane, she took a quick glance down the beach and was reassured to see Todd setting up the stepladder. That was promising; it looked like he knew what he was doing after all.

As Ella reached the top of the steps, she looked along the lane to see a car pull off Libby's drive as Libby stood and waved it off.

"Hello Ella." She gestured for Ella to join her. "Come on over for a minute." Ella jogged across the road and they walked back towards her house.

"I thought it best to leave him to it. Don't think he'd appreciate me watching over him while he paints."

"You're lucky he got there at all."

"Why?"

"I couldn't get him out of bed. I had to shout him up three or four times. I had a good mind to leave him there except I didn't want him to let you down. But he's there now, so that's alright."

They were in Libby's kitchen and she was automatically filling the kettle. Ella turned away and looked out of the window cringing uncomfortably.

"Ella, have a look at these invitations for your birthday do." Libby was holding an invitation delicately between finger and thumb, up to the light. Ella moved to her side and took a look. They were exquisite, hand-made, on heavy cream card with a deep pink sash of satin ribbon along the folded edge. The main body of the card had a raised gold silhouette of a champagne glass with a fine dusting of pink glitter rising to form a cloud of sparkling bubbles.

"Libby, these are beautiful. You must let me know what I owe you for all this."

"Oh, don't worry. A friend of mine has a shop here in the village. I always go to her for cards, invitations, stationery, all that sort of thing and she gives me a good price. I'll write them out for you too, if you like. You'll have to give me a list of all the people you'd like to come." Libby stopped in her tracks. She caught Ella's bewildered look and realised she was completely over-whelming her friend. "It's ok, I'd like to do it, honestly. I've even taken calligraphy lessons at the college – years ago that is."

Ella was interested. "Did you? I've always wanted to do that. Beautiful works of art, some of it."

"Yes, I really enjoyed it. I'd love to do the invites – as long as you don't think I'm taking over."

Ella smiled warmly. She wasn't particularly bothered Libby was taking on the organising of the party, she was more concerned about who to invite. "I'm more than happy for you to do them. As long as – you give me some calligraphy lessons at the same time."

"I'd love to. It's a done deal."

Back in her cottage, Ella sat at the kitchen table with pen and paper. At the top of the page she wrote 'Colette and Simon'. She wanted them to come of course. And then she paused. Her job as a freelance writer was by nature a solitary one and most of her work colleagues she only knew by email or phone. She kept in touch with a couple of girlfriends from school but all it really amounted to was birthday cards and an annual update letter at Christmas. She hadn't seen either of them for years.

Ella put down her pen and gazed out of the window into the garden. She and Jon had had a good social life with a variety of friends from different areas of their lives, mostly from Jon's work, she realised. With hindsight she recognised invitations had began dropping off a while before Jon left. She wondered if he was intercepting them or whether other people had noticed she and Jon were no longer a proper couple – even before she had.

Ella had never felt the need to make friends of her own. Jon had always been enough for her. She looked back at the piece of paper on the table and felt a little guilty that Libby had bought all those beautiful invitations and she was only going to send out one - to Colette and Simon.

Ella looked at the clock, half the morning had gone already and she hadn't done any work yet. She had a few article proposals she wanted to send out and decided to work until lunchtime then she would take Todd something to eat and perhaps then she would speak to him.

At just after one o'clock Ella stepped out into the sunshine finally pleased with her morning's work. She'd made Todd some cheese salad sandwiches and grabbed a bag of crisps and a can of coke from the fridge. As she got to the steps leading down to the beach, she stopped and looked towards the hut. Todd was standing with a girl. Ella looked harder, it looked like Jess, yes it was, and she'd obviously had the same idea and taken him his lunch. They were both tucking into a bag of chips.

Ella turned to return to the cottage. She would give it until a bit later in the afternoon and then pay him a visit.

A loud knock at the back door, mid afternoon, scuppered her plan again. She opened the door and was surprised, and unprepared, to see Todd standing there.

"Hi. Is everything ok?"

"Yeah. I've finished all I can. It'll need another coat but it's got to dry first."

"Ok, great." Ella was taken unawares and was stalling until she could think of a good reason not to let him go.

"Ok, right, payment. Shall I pay you now for today? Or at the end?" Ella was flustered and knew she was babbling nonsensically. And was getting annoyed with herself for it.

"Don't mind," mumbled Todd appearing completely indifferent to the whole money thing, which antagonised her further. She took a deep calming breath. Todd was turning to leave.

"I wanted to speak to you about something." Her voice came out harsher than she intended. Todd turned back to face her, slouched, hands in his pockets, his eyebrows raised in sarcastic defiance, which only served to fuel her determination.

"I found some money here a few weeks ago." She waited for a reaction but nothing. "I wondered if you might know who it belongs to."

Todd shrugged his shoulders. And then as if he couldn't stop himself, he added, "Why would I?"

Ella dug into her jeans pocket for the earring and then remembered she'd removed it for safe-keeping. Where had she put it? Todd followed her glance around the kitchen, wondering what she was looking for. They both spotted it at the same time, on the dresser by the bowl of fruit, the small silver stud in the shape of a skull.

Todd stared, unblinking as Ella picked up the earring between her thumb and forefinger.

"Quite distinctive, isn't it?"

Todd said nothing and his expression gave nothing away. He wasn't sure where this was going or how serious it was going to get.

"It is yours, isn't it?"

He didn't confirm or deny which Ella took as a 'yes'. She closed her hand around the earring.

"You've been using my hut."

Todd just shrugged again.

"You have no right."

"It's not just me! Jess uses it too – all the time. To sneak off with her boyfriend. Where's my money?" he demanded.

"Where did it come from?"

Todd remained stubbornly silent again.

"You stole it?"

"No!" Caught you, she thought.

"So, where did it come from?"

Todd sensed she was not going to give up. He decided to go for damage limitation.

"A mate brings stuff over from France – in his boat."

"Stuff? What sort of stuff?"

Ella was terrified at what she might be caught up in. Todd saw the fear in her face and struggled to stop himself from grinning.

"Just drink, alcohol," he said casually, "not drugs or anything."

Ella felt physically relieved but her anger returned immediately at the sight of his smirking face.

"You're importing alcohol illegally and then what? Who buys it?"

"I don't import it. A mate just brings it over. Just beer and stuff, beer and wine. We sell it to the kids at school. And their parents," he added as if this would somehow lessen his crime. "Anyway, we don't do it anymore," he concluded as a last ditch attempt to save himself.

"Right, so you don't do this anymore? How come?"

"My mate's Dad found out and banned him from the boat."

"Oh." It wasn't the answer Ella wanted. She wanted him to acknowledge the error of his ways and to say he'd learnt his lesson.

"But you would if you could then?"

Todd sighed, what did this woman want – a signed confession?

"No, I wouldn't." He knew what she wanted to hear. "It's not worth the risk – and it doesn't pay that great. I suppose you're gonna tell my Mum?"

Ella wasn't at all convinced the stupid sorry look on his face had anything to do with remorse or concern for his mother's feelings. She didn't answer but leant against the dresser thinking what she should do next. She had envisaged having this conversation with Todd over and over again but had never imagined what the final outcome might be. And now they were here, she wasn't sure which way to go.

Ella was getting weary of this. She wanted to wrap it up. "I'm going to give the money to local charities."

"You can't do that! It's my money!"

"And I won't tell your Mother. Or the police. And you're to tell your sister and your mates that I've changed the lock and my beach hut is out of bounds. You understand me?"

Todd already had the back door open and was on his way out without a word.

"I'll see you tomorrow then at nine-thirty," she said half-heartedly to his back. She closed the door and leaned back against it, shaking, not sure whether Todd would return tomorrow or not, and not sure if she wanted him to.

Todd did return and two days later he had finished painting the hut. Ella had left him to it, not particularly wanting to spend any time in his company. He had shown real anger at not getting his money back but Ella was sure she had done the right thing. The door was open and she called out as she jogged up the steps. Todd was rinsing brushes in the sink and turned towards her as she came in, just about managing to smile. Ella felt perhaps they had reached an understanding and wanted to show she had no hard feelings, and also she was really pleased with what he'd done.

"Todd, it looks gorgeous. Thank-you so much. It's so bright and clean. You've done a fantastic job. I'm really pleased." His smile widened just a little.

Ella delved into her back pocket and pulled out a hundred pounds, offering it to him.

Todd took the money and stuffed it in his pocket, thinking he would much rather have his three and half thousand.

"Just one more thing," said Ella, searching in her pocket again. She opened her hand to reveal the earring. "Here, I think you'd like this back," she said as she dropped it into Todd's palm. "Your sister said you'd probably find it in your pocket!" And then she added, "I hope your girlfriend realises how lucky she is." Todd wasn't sure what she meant by this and came to the conclusion that this odd woman might be a bit lonely, either that or she fancied him.

Chapter Twelve

Ella was getting completely carried away and loving every minute of it. Her trolley was loaded up with pots of paint in shades of pink, new bed linen and matching curtains. On top of that was a delicate beaded chandelier which would sparkle prettily and an unusual gingham effect rug with a border of red rosebuds.

Colette and Simon were coming to stay on the weekend of her birthday and she was going to decorate the guest bedroom ready for them.

After Todd had done such a good job with painting the beach hut, she had been inspired to buy some new furnishings for it and now she couldn't wait to begin on the cottage. She had set off early this morning to avoid the rush hour traffic and had driven into town. A thin layer of cloud blocked the fullness of the sun, allowing just a hazy hint of warmth but the breeze was fresh. It was the sort of day that could go either way. The cloud might thicken and the breeze might grow stronger or it could end up being a scorcher.

Ella struggled to steer her heavy trolley around the corner and then right at the other end of the shop she saw shelves and shelves of fluffy bath towels in all sizes and in every imaginable shade. She couldn't resist and pushed her trolley in that direction. In the next moment she was handling the soft cotton luxuriousness and trying to decide on a colour scheme for her bathroom right there and then. Unable to make up her mind, she settled for a couple of new bath sheets and hand towels in white. It would be nice to put new towels out for Colette and Simon when they came, she justified to herself.

Ella smiled at the sight of her full trolley. She was in good spirits and made her way to the checkout with a nagging feeling that her purchases might not fit into her tiny boot. With no back seat in her car, she might have to squeeze things onto the passenger seat and maybe even drive home with a chandelier on her lap.

Ella paid for her shopping and piled the bags back into the trolley. As she wheeled it across the car park, she spotted someone familiar a short distance from her car. It was Andrew, walking along with a large paper bag tucked under his arm while he searched for his keys in his pocket.

As she got nearer, he turned towards her. "Hello Ella. Been shopping I see."

"Hello Andrew. Yes, and I'm not sure it will all fit in."

"Hang on just a minute and I'll give you a hand." Andrew gave up looking for his car keys and placed the paper bag on top of Ella's car roof.

He helped her stack her shopping into the boot and it was soon evident it was not all going to fit. Ella slammed the boot shut and then Andrew began placing the curtains and towels on the passenger seat. Only the chandelier was left. Andrew tried to balance it on top of everything else but it was too precarious.

"Best if I put this in mine, I think. I'll drop it off later, shall I?"

"Thank-you. That'll teach me to get carried away. It's a good job you were here."

Andrew laughed. "Are you heading home now?"

"Yes, I'll follow you out."

"Well, actually, I was about to dump this lot in the car," Andrew retrieved his bag from the roof, "and go for a coffee and some cake. Would you care to join me?"

"I'd love to." Andrew smiled his lovely smile and Ella thought what a lovely morning this had been and how pleased she was to have run into him.

Ella locked her car and waited while Andrew placed the bag on the back seat of his car. She could see some of its contents; brushes mainly and pencils and tubes of paint.

"You're an artist."

"Well, not really. I dabble, as they say."

"What sort of things do you paint?"

"I'll have a go at anything. I've done a few landscapes but I'd really like to get into portraits. They're the most challenging I think. The skill is not just to copy what's in front of you but to capture the essence of someone's character, maybe the warmth in their eyes or a cheeky slant to their smile, something that belies their real personality."

"What if you don't know them very well?"

"Well, actually, I wouldn't like to paint someone I didn't know to some degree. It would feel just too two-dimensional, you know? That's the fun for me, to capture so much more than the picture in the picture. Do you see what I mean or am I babbling?"

Ella laughed. "No, not at all. I do understand what you mean."

They walked to the edge of the car park and turned onto the high street which was full of seventeenth century timber frame houses, most of which were now employment agencies and estate agents. They all looked the same but every now and then there was an interesting specialist shop. They had just passed one selling an amazing variety of chocolate from all over the world and another selling gifts for the village home and garden. Ella made a mental note to return to this street as soon as she could. They walked along in silence for a while, walking close together.

"There's a splendid little place just down this little alley called The Tea Cosy. I've never tried their tea but it is very cosy."

"Sounds good to me."

"They have a great range of coffee and the most amazing chocolate cheesecake – huge portions."

They turned left into a narrow side street and just a little way down, Andrew stopped outside the tearoom and together they peered in the window. Someone had cleverly produced a very artistic display of dainty and colourful pastries, arranged meticulously in perfectly straight rows. Colourful macaroons in a rainbow of pastel shades, slices of Battenburg cake next to pure white fluffy meringues filled with dark berries.

As Ella suspected they might, black clouds had gathered overhead and the narrowness of the alleyway made it dark outside. The inside of the tearoom was dark too but with subtle lighting making it cosy and inviting.

Andrew went inside holding the door open for Ella. The lady behind the counter recognised him and greeted him with a warm welcome, automatically picking up two menus. "Over by the fire Andrew?"

"Yes please."

Andrew and Ella settled themselves at a small table for two against the open brickwork wall close to a blazing log fire.

"You come here often?" Ella couldn't resist the cliché and they both laughed.

"Libby introduced me to this place actually. She has a taste for the finer things in life, seems to know where all these sorts of places are – and she knows I have a sweet tooth. We come here together some times."

"Are you two -?" Ella paused trying to find the right words. Andrew looked at her with raised eyebrows.

"Are we what?"

"You know. An item. Together?"

"Good heavens, no. She's like a daughter to me. She is my daughter, my daughter-in-law anyway. Mother of my grandchildren and all that."

"Sorry. It's just that, I got the impression you're very close."

"Yes. In a way we are. Oh, Libby, she's a funny woman. She likes everyone to think she's Miss Independent, always in control, capable of everything all at once and phased by nothing."

"Mm, yes, that's the impression I get. She's been very good to me."

"She is good. A good mother. A good friend. But she has a vulnerable side too. She's all brave talk about her marriage break-up and how civilised it all is and how pally they all are. But I know, she doesn't like being on her own. And it took a long time for her to get back on her feet after David moved out. He's got himself a new partner, a nice woman but Libby hasn't really moved on." Andrew paused and looked away out of the window before continuing. "Which is why she tends to, you know, rely on me rather a lot."

Ella smiled and nodded in agreement.

"Let's just say, it's not always convenient." Andrew laughed kindly, his warm chocolate brown velvet eyes looking deep into hers, and that together with his lovely smile and the heat from the burning logs were giving Ella's cheeks a red rosy glow.

The woman from the counter appeared again, holding her notebook and pen and smiling expectantly. Ella quickly picked up her menu, conscious that they hadn't even looked at it yet. She felt a little flustered and looked across at Andrew sitting calmly with his hands folded, resting on his closed menu.

"What are you having?"

"My usual. A Costa Rican coffee and a chocolate cheesecake. I can recommend them.

Ella slapped her menu back down on the table. "I'll have the same."

Andrew and Ella enjoyed a total of three cups of coffee and the rest of the afternoon together. It was still dark when they left the tearoom, heavy grey clouds hung low in the sky and before they had even got to the end of the alley, the skies opened and the rain poured down. It seemed entirely natural for Ella to link arms with Andrew as they ran along, staying close to shop shelters whenever they could.

They each fell into their cars as quickly as possible and waved through the misty windows as they drove off. Somewhere during the journey they got separated and continued their own journeys home.

Elle grabbed the bags from the passenger seat and ran inside, plonking them, dripping wet, on the draining board. She would retrieve the things from the boot later. Despite a couple of soakings and not even minding the droplets of rain which were trickling down her forehead, Ella felt warm and happy inside.

The rain continued for the rest of the afternoon and on into the evening. The cranky heating system meant the house felt cold again and Ella went from room to room shutting the curtains to keep the meagre warmth inside and the chilly draughts out. April was nearly over and it was definitely time for some spring sunshine, she thought. Even so, after a hot bath and while tucking into a bowl of Carbonara, her thoughts on the day were enough to create an inner glow of warmth and contentment.

She reflected on the wonderful afternoon she had spent with Andrew, their easy conversation, his lovely smile and the cosy tearoom. She couldn't help smiling herself.

Andrew had been married twice before. His first wife had died after twenty-five years of marriage leaving two grown up children and him to look after each other. He had married again a couple of years later but this relationship only lasted a couple of years and she left Andrew to be with someone else. Ella remembered Andrew laughing as he told her, 'someone twenty years younger than myself'. Fortunately there were no children from that relationship.

Andrew had mentioned he wasn't really looking for a serious relationship and had joked that at sixty-three, he was too old to even think of 'long term'. Ella had been a little embarrassed, not entirely sure if the comment was directly aimed at her or whether he was clarifying the situation between him and Libby.

Andrew had then asked as honestly and directly as he had spoken, if she had ever been married. Ella was still analysing the moment when she felt her stomach surge and anticipated tears – but they never came, to her relief. For some reason, she didn't want Andrew to know how devastated she had been after Jon left. Briefly and quickly she simply told him the bare facts. Maybe, she hoped, there would be other times to fill in the gaps.

Chapter Thirteen

Libby opened the cardboard box which had just been delivered by the courier company. She scooped out masses of polystyrene packaging and as if she was delving into a lucky dip, she lifted out a packet of red balloons, and a 'Happy Birthday' banner, more balloons and other fancy birthday party paraphernalia. She took a folder from the shelf and filed the delivery note and invoice inside.

Everything was organised as far as it could be for Ella's birthday. Her house was perfectly clean and tidy and the day was Libby's to do what she wanted. Rather presumptuously she had decided to call on Francine to discuss the mid-summer party arrangements. She hadn't seen or heard from Francine for several weeks and thought it best to take matters into her own hands. She also wanted to invite her to Ella's party which meant she needed to speak to her pretty soon.

Libby had already chosen what to wear to Francine's and had laid the outfit on the bed, quite pleased with her choice. She wasn't entirely convinced the cream trousers were right for a woman of her age but this pair was so expensive, she reckoned they ought to come with a guarantee to make the wearer look fabulous, and she was sure she had seen Francine in something similar. Libby ran her fingers over the terracotta silk shirt. She knew this would suit her colouring well.

She picked up the phone and dialled the number from memory. Francine was a busy woman but Libby knew she kept Wednesday mornings free for anything spontaneous.

"Hello?"

"Hello Francine, it's Libby here. Just ringing to see if you're free this morning to go over some of the details for the summer party."

"Oh hello Libby. It's good to hear from you. I know, we do have an awful lot to discuss before August. I'm afraid I can't do this morning. In fact, I'm on my way out now. Ok, if I give you a call back?"

"Yes, of course. But while you're there, I'm giving a party in a couple of weeks for my new neighbour, Ella. It's her birthday but it's more of a welcome to the neighbourhood thing. I'd love you to come, it's on the ...."

"Ah, I'm sorry Libby, I shall be away that weekend, going up to London. Was going to ask you to join us actually. Never mind, another time perhaps. Anyway, the party sounds a lovely idea, typical of you to think of it. Shame I shall have to miss it. Ok, I really must go. Will give you a call tomorrow."

Libby replaced the receiver. She was overwhelmed with disappointment, completely deflated. She plonked herself down on the bed, partly sitting on her new silk blouse which she tugged out from beneath her bottom and tossed to the side of her, not caring that it was all creased now.

Libby sat there and weighed up what was the most disappointing, the fact that Francine had other plans for the morning or the fact that she wasn't able to make Ella's party, that was a real frustration. She had wanted Francine to see what she was really capable of; her catering skills and her flair for organising social events.

A noise downstairs had Libby jumping up from the bed and then she heard Andrew's voice calling out.

"Libby? Are you home?"

"Hi Andrew, I'm coming."

Libby hurried downstairs to find Andrew in the kitchen by the open back door. As she approached, he rattled the handle. "You left the door open."

Libby placed her hands on Andrew's shoulders, stood on tiptoes to reach him and kissed him on his cheek.

"Oh Andrew, shh! You fuss too much." Libby flicked the kettle on and took two mugs from an overhead cupboard, shooting Andrew a sideways glance, and grinning. "But I love you for it!"

Andrew smiled at her but said nothing. Libby was pouring boiling water into the mugs when there was another noise at the door, this time just a gentle tap. Libby and Andrew both looked up to see Ella peering in through the glass smiling at them both. Andrew was there in an instant opening the door to let her in.

Libby spoke first. "Hello Ella, you want tea? We're just having some." Without waiting for an answer, Libby was already reaching into the cupboard for another mug.

"Yes please."

"Hello, how are you?" said Andrew. Libby continued with the tea making.

"Hello Andrew, I'm very well thank-you, and you?"

Libby glanced over her shoulder. Was Ella blushing?

"I saw your car parked outside and thought I might pop by, I hope you don't mind. I wondered if you had my light shade still in your car?"

Andrew smiled right at her. "Yes, I do. I was going to drop it round while I was here."

"Oh, that's kind. Thank-you."

Libby brought the mugs over to the table, feeling for all the world as if she were interrupting something very private and couldn't help feeling a little put out, after all this was her house that she was being made to feel uncomfortable in. She placed the mugs on the table and looked between Andrew and Ella, trying to smile, she hoped, convincingly. For a few moments no-one spoke and then Libby found herself getting impatient.

"Ok, you'll have to explain to me. How does Andrew have your light shade in his car?"

"I was shopping a few days ago and bought much too much and it didn't all fit in my car. Luckily Andrew had parked near me, just happened to be there, and kindly offered to bring the shade back for me. It just wouldn't squeeze in anywhere." Ella felt as though she was excusing herself for something she shouldn't have done. Andrew continued.

"We went to The Tea Cosy." Andrew plucked a carrier bag from the floor, placed it on the table and delved inside. "Which is where I discovered me and Ella share a passion for Motown music." He lifted out a selection of CDs. "So I thought I would bring these over, Libby, thought you might like to use them at Ella's party."

"Thank-you," was all Libby could say. She was unbelievably relieved when Todd entered the kitchen and disturbed the magic in the room. Magic which was between two people and excluded her.

"Hello Todd, love. Been revising for exams?" Libby wanted normality back in her kitchen. Todd took a bottle of milk from the fridge, grunted something vaguely affirmative at his mother and then noticed the two visitors.

"Hello Ella." He watched for her reaction.

"Hi Todd. It's good to see you. How are you?" Todd noticed her wide smile. She seemed really pleased to see him.

"Fine thanks." He was smiling back. And staring.

Libby was dumbstruck; her son had just spoken totally coherently – to someone else. Twice. And he was actually smiling at the same time. She glared at him. "Don't drink that milk out of the bottle."

Ella stood on a chair and fitted the pretty beaded chandelier in place – the final touch to the newly decorated guest bedroom. She'd managed to paint the walls and woodwork in just a couple of days, putting up the soft furnishings as the final touch. Really the carpet needed replacing but that would have to wait for a while. She stepped down and slid the chair back in its place in front of the small dressing table and then switched the light switch on, looking up to admire the pretty effect of the yellow light flickering and sparkling through the glass beads. It looked charming, the whole room did.

Ella switched off the light and turned into the room. It was decorated entirely in white and pink, gratuitously feminine and girly. She loved it. And she knew for a fact Colette would love it too. It would become Colette's room.

She remembered when Colette was a young teenager and had begun to stay over with her and Jon on weekend visits. Colette had chosen her bedroom and they had decorated it together. Wallpapering and painting the woodwork side by side, they were soon giggling when one of them managed to get paint on their nose or in their hair. From that weekend they had developed a loving friendly relationship, not stepmother-stepdaughter but something unique and genuine, special to them both.

Back in the kitchen, Ella picked up a letter from the table and re-read it, quickly scanning to the bottom where Colette confirmed she and Simon would be arriving on Friday evening, Ella's birthday, ready for the party on Saturday. Ella was so looking forward to seeing them both, particularly Colette. It would be lovely to have other people in the cottage and to be able to look after them, fuss them and cook for them. It would be Colette's first visit since Ella had moved in. On a couple of occasions, usually when Ella was feeling a little down anyway, she wondered if perhaps Colette was making excuses to stay away. Maybe she had decided to put distance between them. Perhaps she spent more time now with her father and his new wife and felt it would be disloyal to him to continue their friendship.

As she looked to the signing-off of the letter and its genuine loving words and masses of childish kisses, she knew now all those silly thoughts were complete nonsense.

Chapter Fourteen

Just as Libby got to the top of the stairs, she heard a knock at the back door. "Bugger!" she sighed, irritated. She had finally got into the habit of locking the door after all Andrew's fretting and if this was now one of the kids home from school, having forgotten their key again, she would have some fretting of her own to do. She was trying to get things ready for the party on Saturday and had been baking all morning. The ovens were full and the kitchen a mess. Before cleaning up properly she had become distracted and had gone out to the garden and started to tidy it after the long winter neglect. Thank goodness she had thought to book Mrs O'Brien for Saturday morning to give the downstairs and the bathrooms a thorough going over.

Libby plodded down the stairs, determined not to hurry herself and teach the kids a lesson to remember their keys. She heard more knocking. "Alright, I'm coming! I'm coming!" Libby entered the kitchen and looked across the room to the back door. She was delighted and at the same time horrified to see Francine through the glass. She tried to ascertain the degree to which her kitchen was an absolute mess but didn't want to give herself away and could only sneak a sideways glance at the worktop as she pounced to unlock the door, kicking her muddy garden shoes to the side out of sight.

"Francine, hello, this is a lovely surprise. Come in. You've caught me in the middle of – everything actually. You'll have to excuse the mess."

Francine stepped over the muddy doormat into the kitchen. Libby noticed and made a mental note to always leave her dirty gardening shoes outside the house from now on.

Francine looked about her. "I can see you're busy."

"Well, come on through to the lounge. It's relatively civilised in there. Tea or coffee or a glass of chilled wine?" Libby really hoped Francine would choose the wine option. She suddenly felt in need of a little pick-me-up.

"Coffee would be lovely." Francine settled herself on the sofa, and was picking up a magazine from the coffee table.

Libby flicked on the coffee machine wondering if she could pour herself a sneaky glass of wine without being heard. She opened the fridge and took out the cream, at the same time noting there wasn't an open bottle of wine in there. Sadly she wouldn't be able to pop the cork without being heard and made another mental note to always have a screw top bottle in the fridge for future such emergencies.

A few minutes to herself in the kitchen while the coffee brewed gave her the chance to throw some items into the dishwasher and wipe the worktop properly. She even had time for a quick glance in the mirror to check her hair was ok and that she didn't have any flour or mud on her face. After a quick slick of lip gloss she kept handy in the drawer, she felt much better and more presentable. She would have loved to have been able to quickly nip upstairs and change her clothes, but she reckoned that would just look too silly.

Libby carried in the tray, immediately noticing Francine's outfit. Beautifully cut cream linen trousers and a pastel peach jumper. She couldn't identify the fibre but it was bound to be a natural mix of cashmere and silk or something. It was so fine and skimmed flatteringly over her slim figure.

"You got me thinking the other day Libby. There is an awful lot to do for my summer party and I just haven't had time to give it much thought yet. God, I'm so busy in the next few weeks. Listen, would you mind, and just say if you can't manage it, but would you mind if I passed some more things over to you? Roger is off to some seminar next week in Florence. I'm no fool, I'm going with him on this one. I haven't been shopping in Italy for well over a year. But then he's off to Norway and he can do that one on his own. Too bloody cold for one thing. I've got together with some of the girls that weekend and we're off for a spa treat. No dieting or exercise or any of that rubbish, we're just going for the pampering and good food – lots of it. And then on the top of all that, there's the New York trip to organise. Sometimes I think I need a secretary to help with all this stuff; it's difficult to manage it all on my own all the time."

Libby just sat and stared, speechless. Francine had such an easy glamorous life. How she envied her. She smiled, pleased Francine wanted her to help more with the party but a little bit miffed too that she hadn't been invited along to the spa weekend. She could do with some serious pampering.

"Where do you want me to start?" Libby asked quietly, feeling a twinge of uncertainness as to whether she could cope with everything she was volunteering herself for.

"Well, to be honest Libby, I haven't really given it much thought as yet. In fact, I've hardly had time to do anything, except make a start on this list. Here, I've made a copy for you." Francine passed Libby a sheet of paper and typed at the top were the words, 'Mid-summer Charity Party' in aid of the Little Pebton village hall restoration fund. 20th August, Woodard Lodge. Underneath there were just three bullet points listed; marquee, catering, invites.

"I thought maybe you could add any ideas you might have and then we could get together again, say, in a few weeks time and see how you're doing? How does that sound?"

Libby looked at the rather pathetic list. Before she could even think about adding any ideas of her own, she could think of a couple of dozen items off the top of her head that would need booking and ordering pretty damn quick if there was to be any sort of party at all. Things like the bar, crockery, a band or disco, and entertainment for the children just to start with. She looked across at Francine as she smoothed the linen of her trousers with a tanned hand, nails manicured and painted a rich red, probably just that morning. A collection of gold bangles jangled as she lifted her hand to push back her glossy hair, lifting her face expectantly at Libby.

"There is a lot to do," said Libby quietly.

"Yes. But I know I can leave it all in your more than capable hands." She smiled. It wasn't a question.

Francine added a dash of cream to her coffee taking a few moments to gauge the subtle change of atmosphere. An idea came to mind.

"Libby, before I forget my silly head, and partly the reason for calling by was to invite you to our spa weekend."

"Really?"

"Yes, of course, naturally. I meant to say earlier. You're to be my special guest, as a thank-you for all you're doing for this party thing. My god! I hope you're free that weekend. You are, aren't you?"

"Well, I'll have to check my schedule," said Libby immediately feeling stupid for such a daft response. As if there could possibly be anything in her diary that she wouldn't cancel or abandon for the sake of this invitation.

"Actually Francine," she said, laughing at herself, "I shall make sure I can make it. Now let me have a look at this list." Libby picked up the piece of paper and studied it intently. "Mm, we need to think about booking a marquee and entertainment, the bar and caterers as a matter of priority and once they're all confirmed, we'll look at the guest list and invites. The rest can wait for a little while." Libby grabbed a pen from the table and began scribbling down some notes.

Francine relaxed and breathed a sigh of relief, leaning back into the sofa and sipping her coffee.

Chapter Fifteen

Ella smiled at the generous pile of post on the doormat. Judging from the assortment of coloured envelopes, it looked as though it was mostly cards. She collected them all up, went through to the kitchen and put them on the table before switching the kettle on. While it boiled, she picked up each envelope in turn, trying to guess who it was from, matching hand-writing with post-marks.

It wasn't her birthday until tomorrow, Friday, and she deliberated over whether to cheat and open her cards today. Colette and Simon would be here tomorrow. They had already arranged to go for a meal at the local pub. Despite hitting thirty-seven and much too close to forty, Ella was looking forward to the day. Feeling happy and virtuous now, she decided to save the cards until tomorrow. She collected them up and placed them on the small mantelpiece in front of the kitchen table.

Ella made tea and popped some bread into the toaster. As always, she mentally planned the day ahead, slotting work, chores and other things-to-do into neat time slots.

After breakfast she had a couple of articles to complete. They were for a magazine which focused on life around the coast of Britain. She hoped to get a lot of work from them. This would probably take her up until lunch time and in the afternoon she planned to go shopping for some nice provisions for her guests. The rest of the day she would spend tinkering about in the cottage and making up the newly decorated spare bedroom ready for tomorrow.

Ella had completed her writing quicker than she thought and not being quite ready for lunch decided to take a stroll along the beach. The day had started off fresh and overcast but the clouds had gradually thinned and cleared. Ella could feel the intense warmth of the sun on her head as she strolled close to the water's edge.

It was quiet on the beach, as she would expect, not yet into the summer holiday season and children still at school. Just a few people had spilled out of their offices and shops to enjoy an early lunch on the beach.

Ella continued to stroll, hands tucked into her jeans pockets, passed the row of beach huts, noting which ones were still in need of a bit of renovation and finally passing her own hut, proud to notice it still looked fantastic since Todd's paint job. She turned and walked around the back of the huts and across the beach, up a few steps and then on towards the gift shops and take-aways. It was busier here with more people grabbing something quick to eat. Ella could understand their temptation. The delicious smell of frying onions and sausages surrounded her as she walked. A little further on and she was hit by the sweet waft of vanilla and sugar. A man was selling hot freshly cooked doughnuts from his catering van.

School kids were on their lunch break. Ella watched a group of schoolboys walking towards her. They had come from the fish and chip shop and were all holding open portions of chips which looked to be very hot judging by the way they gingerly took a chip between finger and thumb, dropping it into their mouths and then huffing and puffing to cool it down.

The boys got nearer and then neatly divided and passed by on either side of her, engrossed in their chip-eating and concentrating on balancing their food while walking with heavy school bags.

Suddenly Ella was enveloped in a delicious aroma of hot chips and vinegar. She inhaled deeply and then continued to sniff the air savouring every last delightful whiff. She had reached the chip shop itself and looked inside to see only one person waiting to be served. Ella, unable to resist, went inside and waited her turn. A few minutes later she was strolling back along the beach, the way she'd came, eating hot chips out of an open bag, with a huge pickled onion and a gherkin tucked precariously into the side.

As she walked and ate, she acknowledged to herself how content she felt with the world in that moment and laughed at the idea that a bag of chips, a pickled onion and a gherkin were responsible for all that.

Ella was full well before she'd finished the large portion and had only managed half the pickles. She threw a few random chips out onto the beach, watching as the gulls swooped immediately to snatch them up. Just as she got to the steep steps leading up to the lane, she threw what was left into a bin.

Once indoors, she headed straight for the kitchen sink to wash her greasy hands. The smell of vinegar on her fingers was not so appealing now she'd stuffed herself full.

Ella grabbed some carrier bags from her stock, her handbag and car keys and set off to do some serious shopping. She was going to drive to the retail park, to one of the large superstores where they had a fantastic wine selection. Apparently Simon was a bit of a buff and she thought he might not appreciate her standard cheap plonk. And anyway, she wanted to get something special to celebrate the weekend, her birthday, her first guests in the cottage and the fact that life was definitely getting better.

Ella spent a most enjoyable time slowly wandering up and down the aisles but it wasn't until she was unloading her very full trolley and then repacking it into what seemed like endless carrier bags, she thought maybe she had gone a little over the top. Colette and Simon were only staying for three days and on two of them they would be eating out.

She just about managed to squeeze all the shopping into her little car and by the time she got home she was feeling tired out. As she carted all the bags into the cottage, dumping them on the kitchen floor, she decided once she had put everything away, she would take a quick afternoon nap. She glanced up at the clock. There wasn't much afternoon left. Where had the day gone? Just as Ella had finished unpacking and was stuffing the decent carrier bags back into her reusable stock, she noticed, out of the corner of her eye, the red light shining on the phone indicating someone had left a message.

It was Colette, sounding rather serious, asking Ella to call her back as soon as possible.

"Colette, it's me, Ella. Is everything ok?"

"Oh Ella, I'm glad you rang back so quick. We're not going to be able to come to your party. I'm really sorry. It's Dad, well not Dad exactly – Danielle." Colette paused and took a deep breath. "The baby's been born. Just this morning, and there are complications. They're not sure if she'll be ok. Dad's in a state. And he's asked me to stay." Another pause. "Ella? Are you still there?"

Ella swallowed hard. "Mm."

"Are you ok? I'm really sorry not to be able to come. You do understand?"

"Yes, of course. It's perfectly understandable that you should want to be with your father at a time like this." Ella was aware she sounded stuffy and formal but it was all she could manage.

Neither knew what to say and the few seconds of silence seemed much longer to both of them. Colette spoke first, barely above a whisper as if the quieter she spoke, the less painful the words would be.

"I have to go Ella, I'm calling from the hospital. I'd better get back to Dad."

"Yes, of course. You get back. I'll speak to you soon."

"Yes, and I'll come up to see you, Ella, as soon as I can. I'm really sorry about this weekend though."

Ella gently replaced the receiver; her breathing had become shallow with fear, fear of her thoughts and her consequent reactions. She stood motionless in front of the phone, her fingers gently fiddling with the necklace at her throat. Inside she was raging. Her ex-husband's baby had been born the day before her own birthday; now there was a date she would never be able to forget.

A girl. He had a daughter. Ella turned away from the phone and walked over to the window which looked out to sea. She corrected herself, Jon now had two daughters. It was hardly the same though. Colette was here before she had met Jon, before she had fallen in love with him, married him and made a home with him. A home in which she expected to fill with children with him.

And he had dropped the bombshell. He didn't want any more children. He'd gone to great lengths to convince her he was right. He never succeeded but she had accepted that was how things were. She had made a choice, and allowed him to take away her dream because she loved him and wanted to be with him. On a certain level, she had been able to accept it all, life was full of difficult choices but what she couldn't accept, on any level, was that he had taken her dream away and given it to someone else.

Ella felt her breath catch in the back of her throat and swallowed hard. She would not cry. She turned back towards the kitchen, hands on hips, trying to be practical, thinking what she should do with herself for the rest of the day. There was no point in putting the finishing touches to the guest bedroom now or tidying and shooshing the rest of the cottage. And there was no point in saving this expensive bottle of wine she had bought especially for the weekend. Ella unpicked the foil wrap and blindly rummaged in the drawer for a corkscrew as tears filled her eyes. She popped the cork and filled a large glass full, almost to the top.

She flopped into the oversized armchair by the window, feeling small and insignificant, looking out and drinking the wine.

Ella had lost track of time. The central heating had switched on, she had drunk over half the bottle of wine and was feeling very warm. The sun was going down and the light was fading. Impulsively she decided to go for a walk along the beach to get some fresh air, and clear her head of the horrible jumble of thoughts that had been torturing her for however long she had been sitting there.

Ella left the cottage in a hurry before she could change her mind. She had pulled on a pair of plimsolls and only a light jacket and once outside, was soon very aware of how inadequate they both were.

Heavy grey clouds were rolling across the sky. Ella looked beyond the sea to the horizon where it was impossible to distinguish the two as they merged into a hard grey darkness. The wind had picked up and was tugging and whipping at her flimsy jacket as she tried to hold it firm to her by digging her hands deep into the pockets. She wanted to walk close to the water and refused to move away from it despite the spray that stung her face as the waves hurled into the air before slamming onto the beach. She was getting colder and colder but for a while she didn't care and then finally after a particularly strong wave washed over her shoes soaking her feet, she veered away from the water's edge.

Suddenly it started to rain and in an instant, it was pouring. Heavy, cold and hard drops battered onto her head as she tucked in her chin. She started to cry. Totally exposed, in the middle of the beach, Ella ran as hard as she could towards the row of huts seemingly miles away in the distance. She clutched the bunch of keys in her pocket. It felt to Ella as though it were raining even harder. She was sobbing now, running blindly in the darkness desperate to reach the shelter of the beach hut.

She had reached the row of huts which offered a little protection. With her head still bent low against the wind, she finally arrived at her hut. She looked up to mount the steps but then jumped back terrified, almost falling backwards down the steps. Someone was there right outside her door hiding in the shadows. Ella didn't have the energy to run away. She just stood there crying, not even looking at or guarding herself from the stranger although she did register that whoever it was, had a large dog with them which was now growling at her.

"Ella? Is that you?"

Ella felt relief at hearing a woman's voice and although she didn't recognise it, felt even more relief that whoever it was did recognise her. She looked up and dared to walk back up the steps towards the woman. She had stopped crying but a single stray sob escaped and it sounded like a cross between a hiccough and a snort. Ella felt slightly embarrassed.

"Ella, what on earth is wrong? It's me Libby."

Ella recognised the voice now and could have fallen at her feet in relief and gratitude at the realisation that it was her friend. Impulsively, she made the very slightest move to reach out and hug Libby but the moment was already gone and she stayed where she was.

"Come up here, out of the rain," said Libby gently. "I was out walking Bonzo and suddenly the heavens opened, we were soaked in no time. I thought we could shelter here until it passed, but it's showing no sign of stopping." Libby paused.

"What were you doing out here Ella?"

"Just walking."

Libby could only just hear her above the hammering of the rain on the beach hut roofs.

"As soon as it eases, we'll go back to mine for a nice cup of tea and I made a fruit cake this afternoon, we'll have a big chunk of that too and get ourselves warmed up in front of the fire." Libby could sense something was seriously wrong but without knowing what and not being able to talk above the noise of this atrocious weather, she relied on the old tried and tested clichés of tea and cake to bring some comfort to her friend.

"We could go inside," said Ella still quietly.

"Pardon?"

"Inside the hut – I've got the key."

"Have you? Well yes, that's a good idea. We'll go inside."

Ella didn't move. She had started to shiver.

"Ella? You said you've got the key? Shall I take it and unlock the door?"

Ella took the bunch of keys from her pocket and with her hand shaking, gave them to Libby to deal with. Libby took them and quickly unlocked the door. She took hold of Ella's arm, firmly but gently and guided her inside. She closed the door and switched on a small table lamp, at the same time instructing Bonzo to lie still on the rug by the door which he did immediately.

Libby took a few seconds to gather herself. She had got wet and cold and had been sheltering outside for a while debating whether to wait it out or make a run for it. Ella had sat down and was shivering violently. Libby looked about her for a way of warming them up. There was only a small oil radiator which she knew would take ages to get going.

Libby put the kettle on and took two large mugs from the cupboard. She kept her thick jacket on and zipped up but looking across at Ella, she could see the thin cotton summer jacket she was wearing was soaked through. Libby sat beside her.

"Come on Ella, take this jacket off. We need to get you warmed up."

Ella tried to unfasten the few small buttons but her hands were still shaking and her fingers were numb.

Libby took over and once she had undone the buttons, Ella managed to wriggle out of the jacket which Libby took from her and hung over the back of a chair. She grabbed a neatly folded blanket from the back of the sofa behind Ella, shook it out, then swiftly folded it in half to make a triangle shawl which she placed around Ella's shoulders. Ella gratefully pulled it tighter around her, she leaned back and tried to relax from shivering.

Libby returned to making the tea. She found teabags and some milk powder, and carried the mugs over to the small table in front of where Ella was sitting. She could see Ella's shivers had not yet subsided and placed her mug on the table then sat down beside her. Ella leaned forward and carefully placed her hands either side of the mug, trying to absorb some of its warmth. She looked up at Libby, her sad little face red and blotchy from the cold and crying. She smiled and Libby smiled back. Ella tried to organise her thoughts into some sort of order. She sipped some tea and then took a deep breath.

Chapter Sixteen

Ella awoke early on her birthday. The sun was shining through the thin curtains giving the whole room a magical glow. She breathed deeply and stretched a little, not ready yet to leave the cosiness of her bed. She looked across the room to where her dress was hanging on the wardrobe door and smiled; it was a beautiful dress. Libby had taken her to a couple of local boutiques and Ella had fallen in love with this one at first sight. It was quite a simple style; sleeveless, knee-length but quite closely fitted subtly showing off her perfect figure. Pale grey fine cotton lawn with splashes of large white flowers. Bright fuchsia pinks and purples were too bold for Ella but she was determined to go for something other than black.

Still smiling at her dress, Ella realised how much she was looking forward to wearing it. She sat up, propping her pillows behind her and leant back again. Ella closed her eyes and waited, preparing herself for the onslaught of feelings and emotions which were bound to descend after the events of the last twenty-four hours.

But nothing happened. She opened her eyes again, surprised that actually she felt ok. Maybe it was the ten hours of solid sleep she'd had.

Libby and Ella had stayed in the beach hut for a couple of hours, sitting out the storm, talking and drinking tea. Ella had poured her heart out and Libby had listened, without interruption. At last the rain had stopped and they walked back along the sodden beach together. They reached Ella's cottage first and Libby insisted on seeing her inside to make sure she was ok. While Ella ran a hot bath, Libby made her yet another cup of tea and a plate of sandwiches and insisted she ate them all up, and as she was leaving, made Ella promise faithfully to go straight to bed after her bath. Ella had been too exhausted at the time to argue against being bossed about by Libby. But that was unfair. Libby wasn't being bossy, she was being a good friend; caring and kind. And in loyalty to Libby and her kindness, Ella did exactly as she was told; she took her bath and was in bed before ten o'clock.

Ella fully expected to awake this morning feeling awful with a throbbing headache at the very least. She always got a headache when she cried -whatever the reason. And being such a private person, she suspected she would feel regret at having revealed all, right from the depths of her heart and soul. She had talked to Libby about everything; the decline of her marriage, Jon not wanting children, him starting a family with someone else, his baby being born yesterday, and how she, even after all this time, still couldn't cope with it all.

But in fact, the reality was she didn't feel any of these things. She felt calm, her head was clear and she had no feelings of regret about talking to Libby. And the most amazing thing was that she was able to think of the little baby girl who had come into the world just yesterday without the usual accompanying stabbings of anger and jealousy. She hoped the baby was out of danger, and that all would be ok.

All of a sudden Ella swung her legs out of bed and got up. She wanted to look in the mirror. Her logic said that as she felt alright, the law of fairness would dictate she must look bloody awful. But no, if it could talk, the mirror on her bedroom wall would say she was definitely the fairest of them all. She looked radiant. Her skin was smooth, fresh and clear, her cheeks had a healthy rosy glow and even her eyes which she fully expected to be red, sore and piggy looking, were bright and clear.

She gave the mirror one last look of satisfaction. "Mm, I must get drunk and drenched more often!"

A loud urgent knock on the front door had Ella grabbing her dressing gown and putting it on as she ran down the steep, narrow stairs, concentrating to not fall down them. She unlocked and opened the door as quick as she could to be met by the biggest bouquet of flowers she had ever seen. It was so big she couldn't even see the person behind them, only the two hands trying to hold them steady. An elderly man stuck his head to the side "Ella Peters?" he said, a big smile on his face.

"Yes," Ella's smile was equally big. "Thank-you." The man handed over the bouquet. "It's a pleasure," he said as he turned and walked slowly back down the drive to his van.

Ella took the flowers into the kitchen and laid them on the table which they almost covered, end to end and side to side. She stood looking at them in their cellophane wrapping, tied with a large bow in yellow and green ribbon. She was wondering who they were from and plucked the mysterious little envelope off the corner, savouring the anticipation. There was no-one obvious she could think of who would make such a grand gesture. She read the card, 'Have a very Happy Birthday. Enjoy your day, kindest wishes, Andrew.'

"From Andrew", she whispered to herself, surprised and delighted he had done such a lovely thing. What a wonderful start to the day. Ella put the kettle on and looked for her vases at the back of the cupboard. She would need all of them to accommodate all these flowers.

Ella made tea and decided on the spur of the moment to treat herself to a special birthday breakfast; a full-on fry-up. Why not? She took it with her cup of tea and ate on the big comfy armchair in the corner of the kitchen from where she could enjoy the view of the flowers on the table.

She spent the rest of a very enjoyable morning taking her time arranging the masses of flowers and positioning them around the cottage. When she had finished, there were flowers in every room.

Back in the kitchen again, Ella sat at the table and opened all her cards. Just as she finished, the phone rang.

"Hi Ella, it's me. Just wanted to wish you a happy birthday." Colette sounded tired and weary.

"Hi Colette. Thank-you. How are you all doing?"

"Baby is doing really well. She's gorgeous and really sweet –." Colette stopped short. "I'm sorry Ella, I wasn't thinking."

"It's ok Colette, really. I'm glad she's doing well. That's very good news. And how is your father today?"

Colette sighed wearily. "He's not so good. He's not been well for a while and he's been kept in overnight. He's having some tests today."

"Oh." Ella was surprised. Jon was hardly ever ill and certainly not one to make a fuss especially if there were other people to look after. Perhaps he was beginning to feel his age, reasoned Ella to herself. All the excitement of a new baby was obviously too much for him. Out of the corner of her eye, Ella noticed Libby coming up the garden path.

"Listen, Colette, I must go, there's someone at the door." It sounded like a feeble excuse to get away, Ella realised. "Shall I call you tomorrow? What time will you be home from the hospital?"

"I'll be home by nine."

"Ok, I'll phone you then. Take care."

Libby, smiling, tapped on the glass at the back door into the kitchen and let herself in.

"Happy birthday to you!" She gave Ella a quick peck on the cheek. "How are you today? You look well." Ella had been a little worried that yesterday's deluge of revelations might affect the balance of their friendship. She didn't regret confiding in Libby but she didn't want to be constantly fussed like a wounded bird either. She needn't have worried.

"Mm, you don't look bad for a thirty-eight year old!" said Libby.

"I'm thirty-seven!" protested Ella.

"Oh yes. Ignore me, I'm just jealous. Here you go, this is for you." Libby handed over a very chic gift bag. Ella peeked inside and lifted out a beautiful silk scarf in pretty delicate shades of grey and blue and peach.

"Thank-you Libby, it's gorgeous."

"You're very welcome," said Libby suddenly noticing the huge vase of flowers on the window cill. "Wow! Who are they from?"

"From Andrew," replied Ella, still delighting in his kindness. She couldn't help but notice Libby's raised eyebrows and wasn't sure how to interpret the expression, but something warned her against telling Libby there were about ten other vases around the house.

"That was nice of him, very typical of Andrew. Just the sort of thing he would do," said Libby. Ella didn't comment. She felt ever so slightly miffed at how Libby's compliment to Andrew had taken away some of the magic of what he had done. She smiled but said nothing.

Fresh out of the oven, the hot sausage rolls wouldn't all fit onto the plate. There was one left over and to plonk it on top would spoil the display so Libby popped it into her mouth. She squeezed the plate into a space on the table and took a second to admire the feast before her. It had taken a lot of time and effort but she was pleased with the results. It looked perfect. She'd got Todd and Jess to put up the red balloons and had put some vases of bright fresh flowers around the place. Her two children hadn't moaned about being expected to be at the party but even more amazing was that Todd looked clean and in fact, rather smart in his new jeans and trendy black shirt. And he was being incredibly helpful, Libby realised. She watched him, a little puzzled, over the other side of the room paying considerable attention to ensuring a 'Happy Birthday' banner was in place and level. Either he had done something for which he felt guilty and which would undoubtedly come to light, or he was after being allowed to do something and was attempting to accrue some advance brownie points.

A sudden commotion in the kitchen snapped Libby out of her pondering. She would think about this later, she decided, and went to see what all the fuss was about.

Andrew had arrived and was forcibly waltzing an unwilling Jess around the kitchen, except she was giggling so hard, she couldn't actually protest. He finally released her as Libby walked in.

"Grandad, you're mad!" said a red-faced, breathless Jess.

"Well, that's charming. I was doing you a favour, teaching you to waltz. You'll thank me one day." Andrew was grinning. Jess had just about managed to regain her composure.

"Yeah right!" She rolled her eyes at her mother and went in search of sausage rolls. Whether or not it was mother's intuition, Libby read her thoughts.

"Don't touch the food. Leave it until at least some guests have arrived."

"The place looks lovely, Libby," said Andrew.

"And so do you Andrew." Libby smiled flirtatiously, taking in his tall, strong build, shown off to maximum effect by a close fitting black polo-shirt style sweater. A couple of buttons were undone which drew Libby's eyes, noticing his tanned neck. His sleeves were pulled up a little revealing strong forearms. Altogether Andrew was in fine form for a man in his early sixties. Libby felt very glad he was there.

A tapping on the window marked the arrival of the first guests. Edwina entered the kitchen; a friend of Libby's from the WI. She was a blustery woman, equally good at flower arranging and gossiping. And her unlikely companion who she must have met on the way was Neil Cookson, the local GP. Tall, slim and looking rather gorgeous in his off-duty casual attire thought Libby. He was also looking rather the perfect partner for Ella she thought, smiling deviously at her sudden brilliant idea. Libby greeted them warmly and served them their first drink, encouraging them to come back and help themselves whenever they wanted. She didn't want to be barmaid all night. She was just wondering how come Todd hadn't been hovering around the booze yet when he appeared in the kitchen to see who had arrived. A knock at the front door signalled the arrival of more people. Jess yelled from the lounge that she would get it.

"What we need now, is for the birthday girl to arrive," said Andrew. "Shall I walk over and see if she's ready?"

"I'll go, if you like?" volunteered Todd. Andrew and Libby looked at Todd and then at each other, eyebrows raised, agreeing silently that this was rather odd. Before either of them had a chance to respond, Ella appeared at the back door, smiling at everyone as she let herself in. She looked lovely. Libby couldn't help but stare, remembering the day they went shopping together for the dress. She was wondering why she hadn't seen the dress first for herself and then felt deflated as she acknowledged the reality of being several inches shorter than Ella and much lumpier around the middle. She felt a pang of jealousy and then immediately felt ashamed of herself.

"Come on Ella, let's get you a birthday drink. There's champagne in the fridge but we'll save it until a bit later. Let's get the party going first." Libby poured a very large glass of white wine for Ella and feeling a particular need, poured an equal measure for herself.

The three of them stayed chatting in the kitchen for quite some time. Despite Libby sensing the house filling with guests, she was reluctant to mingle and welcome them even though she knew she should. Finally, she had no choice when Jess, the designated front door monitor, appeared, to say there was a group of teenagers hovering outside the front garden who she didn't recognise. Libby looked across to Andrew hoping he would instinctively volunteer to deal with the situation but he was engrossed with Ella, telling her some highly amusing anecdote or other judging by her uncontrollable giggling. A little irritated, Libby marched out of the kitchen to deal with the gatecrashers herself.

More guests continued to arrive and Libby tried to meet and greet them in the kitchen, helping them to a drink. Todd was still hanging about in there, surreptitiously pretending to load the dishwasher with glasses, secretly but not very discreetly emptying their contents beforehand. Libby gave him a look but she was feeling a little overwhelmed by everything and weary of it all already. As long as Todd behaved, she didn't have the energy to be angry with him. She was getting angry with Andrew and Ella though, for staying in the kitchen this long. She shot Andrew a look which obviously did the trick, much to her relief.

"I suppose we ought to mingle for a bit," said Andrew.

Ella grimaced indicating she'd rather stay where she was.

"It is your party after all, I shouldn't keep you all to myself. Let's go through, I'll introduce you to some people."

It was some time later before Ella returned to the kitchen, hot and thirsty. She poured herself a glass of water from the tap. She was having a fantastic time and couldn't believe she had actually been dancing, with everyone.

She thought she was alone in the kitchen and jumped when Todd suddenly appeared close behind her.

"Do you want a proper drink?"

"Oh, hello, I didn't see you there Todd. You should be in there, having a dance."

As she spoke, the music changed to a much slower tempo; someone had put on a CD of romantic love songs. Todd slid his hands around her waist.

"We could dance together here." Instinctively Ella tried to gently back away but was blocked by the kitchen sink behind her. Instead she turned and rinsed her glass, placing it upside down on the drainer. Ella smiled.

"That might look a bit odd, don't you think?"

"I don't care," said Todd a little petulantly. He let his hands drop from her waist but stayed where he was, almost as though he didn't know what else to do with himself. Ella made a move to quickly squeeze past him which only made things worse as Todd seized the moment and put his hands around her again and gently but firmly pulled her towards him and aimed to kiss her right on the mouth. Just in time, Ella turned away but Todd only proceeded to kiss her clumsily on her neck.

"Todd! For goodness sake!" Ella freed herself, just as Andrew walked into the kitchen. He weighed up the situation immediately and trying to make light of it, he simply said, "Hello, I've got competition have I?"

Ella, bright red, glared at him. She was cross with Todd but didn't want to hurt his feelings. But it was already too late. Todd, also bright red, pushed passed his grandfather and fled out of the room.

"Oh Andrew, that was a bit insensitive."

"Not as insensitive as you giving him the brush off!" He was smiling as he spoke.

"What was I supposed to do? Let him kiss me?"

"Not let yourself be alone with him in the kitchen? The poor boy's been mooching around you all evening."

Ella was still indignant. "Well, I didn't realise that. And I didn't even know he was in here. I only came in for a glass of water." Ella raised her hand to her cheek, it was burning. She wasn't sure if it was due to the alcohol or embarrassment. Andrew was still laughing but gently now. He bent his knees a little so his face was on a level with hers, he had an irresistible kindness in his eyes. He placed his hands on Ella's waist just as Todd had done but with Andrew it was a very welcome and exciting gesture.

"He will get over it Ella. I promise there'll be no lasting damage. With the amount of lager he's been supping, he probably won't even remember tomorrow."

Ella felt a little better. "I need some fresh air."

"Good idea, shall we go for a walk, or would you rather be alone?"

"No, I don't want to be alone. I seem to get myself in trouble. Let's go for a walk along the beach, that'll be lovely."

"Ok, but I can't guarantee you won't get into trouble!" Andrew grinned and winked at her wickedly. "One second –." He pulled open the fridge door and took out a bottle of champagne. "Time for this, I think."

"Oh, I'm not sure. Libby might not like us just taking it."

"She shouldn't mind – I bought it. Come on, quick."

Ella grinned back, feeling like a naughty teenager sneaking off with their forbidden stash.

It was refreshingly cool down on the beach. Ella slipped off her sandals and walked barefoot, feeling the cold, damp sand between her toes. They walked together slowly side by side in easy companionable silence.   Ella smiled to herself; here she was going for a walk by moonlight, barefoot along the beach with the loveliest of men who had that morning, sent her the biggest bouquet ever and was holding in his hand a chilled bottle of champagne. Six months ago, she never would have believed this could ever happen.

As if he'd read her thoughts, Andrew lifted the bottle of champagne and said, "I didn't bring glasses." They both laughed.

"It's ok, I have some in the hut, it's just over there."

"Ah yes, the famous beach hut, I've been looking forward to seeing this."

"Have you indeed? Here we are, it's this one here. Oh! Guess what?"

"What?"

"I don't have the keys with me!"

Again, they both laughed at the silly hopelessness of their situation, although this time, their laughter was a little less carefree, tinged by a pang of disappointment that they couldn't get into the beach hut, be alone and drink champagne together. Ella sat down heavily on the step. Andrew joined her.

"We could drink from the bottle?" he suggested.

"Mm." Ella wasn't so keen.   Sitting on the step swigging champagne from the bottle wasn't the romantic setting she had in mind. Andrew took her hand in his, lifted it to his mouth and kissed it gently. Just a short while ago, they'd set off for their beach walk with no more plan than to get a breath of fresh air, but now the idea of being together in the hut had been formed, it was impossible to let it go.

Andrew continued to hold her hand, brushing it against his cheek. Ella stared straight ahead to the darkness of the sea and the stars twinkling overhead. She turned to look at Andrew, and smiled gently which did nothing to express the intense longing she felt for him.

"Think of something," she whispered. Andrew didn't need telling twice. He'd already spotted a small rock which would easily knock the padlock from the door.

"Hold this." He handed her the champagne bottle and picked up the rock from the sand. He tapped it against the padlock gently at first, conscious of not causing too much damage, and then one final heavy blow opened the padlock sending it whizzing across the floor.

Ella picked it up and placed it on the railing post as Andrew went inside. She followed him in and automatically pulled the door shut behind her, closing out the rest of the world. The room was dark except for the glow from the moon, creating a slightly eerie atmosphere. Ella didn't like it and shivered. Andrew put his arms around her and pulled her close. The warmth of his body and the strength and security of his arms around her made her feel better immediately. As Andrew kissed her, Ella thought her legs would give way completely. Instinctively, she reached up and folded her arms firmly around his neck pulling them even closer together.

Even after the kiss had finished, she didn't want to let him go. They stood locked together in the silent, semi-darkness, Ella wondering what would happen now but not knowing what to say.

She didn't really relish the idea of moving over to the tiny bench seats, it would take all their concentration to not fall off. Ella pictured Andrew going up the loft ladder and for a second worried in case he wasn't able to make it. The thought brought a big smile to her face, which Andrew could see, and she gave a little giggle.

"What are you laughing at?"

Any awkwardness she had felt a few moments ago had disappeared now.

"I was just wondering if you could make it up the ladder, you don't have a weak heart do you? Or dodgy knees?"

Andrew looked over his shoulder towards the loft. "Is that where the bed is?"

Ella nodded, still smiling.

"Right. I'll show you how dodgy my knees are." And then a little more seriously, "But I have no idea what's going on in my heart at the moment." He kissed her lightly on the forehead and then went up the ladder first and helped Ella up beside him.

Much later, after they had both been dozing for a few minutes, Andrew looked across at Ella lying in his arm. "That's a pretty smile. Do you wake like that every morning?"

Ella twisted around to lean on Andrew's broad, grey-haired chest.

"I might from now on. And it's not quite morning so I reckon we should both be getting back to the party. It would be terribly rude not to go back at all."

"I suppose you're right – shame, I was quite comfortable."

"I know, I could stay here all night."

They began dressing, retrieving items of clothing from where they had been dropped.

"I have an idea," said Andrew. "Let's go back for a while, say our good-byes, then I'll walk you home but we'll do a detour and come back here. What do you say?"

"That's a fantastic idea. Do you mean it? Shall we really do that?"

Andrew laughed, Ella was like an over-excited child.

"If you want to, then we will."

Back at Libby's house, the party was in full swing. Someone had cranked the music up and they could hear it before they even reached the driveway. Ella and Andrew separately hoped they could slip back in unnoticed but unfortunately they walked in on a commotion in the kitchen.

Libby was holding open the fridge door accusing a very wobbly Todd of pinching a bottle of champagne, which he was denying with as much strength as his swaying body would allow. He turned, saw Ella and Andrew and turned back to leave the room, banging into the doorframe on his way.

Libby pushed the fridge door shut. Ella and Andrew just stood there waiting for the fallout as to where they had been. They looked at Libby and she looked back at them, swaying a little herself.

"Well, some bugger's gone and pinched the champagne! What do you think of that?" Without waiting for a reply, Libby swivelled on one foot and went back to the party.

Ella and Andrew shared a colluding look; relieved that they hadn't been missed. Unbeknown to them, they were having the same thought, how quickly could they get away again?

Chapter Seventeen

Todd woke early with a thumping headache and a raging thirst and went down to the kitchen. The house was still in a bit of a mess although his mum had dealt with the worst of it last night by stacking things ready for the dishwasher. He opened the fridge and took out a bottle of mineral water and drank almost half its litre contents, noticing the left-over sausage rolls in there. He took a handful, closed the door with his foot and popped a sausage roll into his mouth closely followed by another. He wandered around the kitchen eating and studying the remains of other leftover food, but it was all cake and soggy battered prawns, nothing of interest to him. He felt better already but jumped nearly out of his skin when the dogs barked as he came into their view from their bed by the door. The shock jarred his head which started pounding again. They danced into the kitchen, skitting around his legs. "Quiet you animals!" Todd bent over to ruffle their ears but as the blood rushed to his head, he stood up again immediately, feeling quite dizzy and realising it was going to be a while before he felt back to normal today.

Betsy yelped at being ignored for a mere fraction of a second. Todd patted her head and filled two random bowls with dried food from a large sack by the door. He didn't really think they were dog bowls but his brain wasn't functioning properly enough to care. He had a vague feeling he would be made to care a bit later on.

Todd knew, that now he had disturbed them, the dogs wouldn't settle and keep quiet if he left them alone. His mother probably wouldn't be too pleased to be woken just yet and it might also lead to a confrontation which Todd certainly wasn't ready for. He hadn't attempted to recall last night's party in any serious detail yet but he had a feeling he hadn't behaved very well. No doubt, he would have to face that later.

While the dogs were concentrating on their breakfast, Todd dashed upstairs and dressed quickly. He didn't bother washing or tidying his hair which was squashed and flat on one side and kinky and sticking out on the other.

Back downstairs, he let the dogs out into the back garden before taking their leads from the hook. To let them see him with their leads in his hand would have them yelping and jumping around the kitchen like mad animals. They walked to heel as Todd crossed the lane and then they were off, down the steps and onto the beach. Todd took a swig of water. Some of it missed his mouth and trickled down his neck which was quite refreshing. He was already looking forward to a long, hot shower when he got back.

The dogs had run on far ahead and on another day, Todd would have run to catch up with them. But today, he didn't have the energy and he didn't think his thumping head could take it. He looked up, the dogs had disappeared from sight. They were in amongst the beach huts. Todd whistled them back but they didn't come, so he quickened his pace to catch them up. He reached the row of beach huts and looked over at Ella's one. His paintwork still looked good. He had enjoyed doing it, especially when Ella started being really nice to him. She hadn't grassed him up to his mum and for that he'd tried to do an especially good job. It was like they had a special secret between them. And then she'd gone and humiliated him, in front of everyone. At first he thought she'd purposely followed him out to the kitchen, how stupid was he? And because of her, Grandad had laughed at him. He wouldn't forgive him for that. Or her. He'd been hanging around Ella all evening. As if he had any chance with her. Old man.

Coming closer to Ella's hut, he noticed the padlock wasn't on the door. A little further on, he could see two tails wagging from behind the hut. The dogs were quiet which probably meant they were up to no good but he decided to take a chance and leave them there for a minute. The hut didn't look damaged in any way but even so he went up the steps and then saw the padlock had been placed on the railing post. It was broken, probably smashed off by the rock he'd just spotted on the floor by the door.

Praying the dogs wouldn't choose this precise second to bark, Todd crept to the door, gently turned the handle and pushed it open. And then he couldn't move; he couldn't believe his eyes.

"Champagne for break-fast. This is totally decadent," said Ella, chinking glasses with Andrew. He was half dressed but had no top on yet while all Ella had to cover her modesty was a small tartan blanket she'd wrapped around her, sarong-style.

"Todd! What are you doing here?" She was confused and struggled to get her thoughts in order. For a brief moment she thought Todd had been sent there to catch them out. But that was ridiculous. Ella looked at Todd expecting him to say something but everyone was silent. Todd was looking at the champagne bottle on the table, vaguely recollecting his mum accusing him of taking it. Ella noticed the direction of his gaze and immediately felt guilty for not owning up last night.

Todd's head was pounding in rhythm with his pulse, it felt like it might explode. Suddenly the dogs barked and Todd turned just as they bounded up the steps. He took the thankful opportunity to get the hell out of there, running passed the dogs and down the steps whistling to them to follow. He ran back up the beach as fast as he could.

Andrew pulled his sweater over his head.

"I feel guilty," said Ella.

"Well you shouldn't. He has a teenage crush on you, that's all. He'll be alright. He'll probably be more angry with me. Are you bothered he might tell Libby about us?"

"Sort of. For some reason. Are you?" Ella noticed his reference to 'us' and couldn't help but feel a tingle of excitement.

"Not really. It shouldn't be a problem. We're not doing anything wrong. But then again things don't always pan out how they should."

"No." Ella knew that well enough.

"Shall we be discreet?" Andrew smiled his big smile which took over his whole face, his kind eyes twinkling.

"Yes, let's."

Andrew left first and Ella was left to secure the hut with a long piece of string which she looped round and round the latch, knotting it several times.

She felt tired and her eyes were heavy but despite this she was smiling remembering the happy reason for her sleepless night.

Chapter Eighteen

Libby stopped sweeping the non existent leaves from the lawn and knowing she couldn't be seen, stood and watched as Dr Cookson let himself out of Ella's cottage and got into his flashy little sports car, very similar to Ella's. Libby smiled to herself; there for a start was one thing they had in common. She'd been very pleased to see them having a dance together at the party just as she had hoped. They looked good together thought Libby, pleased with herself.

Libby was convinced it was providence itself that had brought Ella down with a stinking cold a few days after the party. Libby had no qualms about ringing the surgery. She was on very good terms with the receptionist and easily managed to secure a home visit by the doctor to her neighbour. Libby checked her watch, he'd been in there for a good twenty minutes. A very positive sign, she thought.

Ella lay in her bed feeling very sorry for herself. She thought it very unfair that she'd been struck down with this vicious cold after she'd been on such a high since her birthday.

She had gone to Libby's the day after the party to help with the cleaning up, but by the middle of the afternoon she was feeling groggy. Libby phoned the following morning and as soon as she heard Ella try to speak she went over to her cottage to take charge. Ella was extremely grateful to Libby for phoning the surgery and for waiting until Dr Cookson arrived. Unfortunately the antibiotics he had prescribed for her chest infection had caused a bad stomach reaction and Ella, still weak, had to request another home visit.

Before he left, he commented on Ella's formidable collection of books on numerous bookcases around the house, and was particularly interested in the very old copy of 'Sailing around the British Isles' which he asked to borrow. She felt an immediate connection to anyone who shared her love of books and told him to pop by anytime he wanted to borrow something which she now hoped wouldn't be misconstrued in any way.

Ella leaned back against the pillows and listened to Neil Cookson's footsteps going down the stairs. At the back door, he bumped into someone else arriving and Ella froze at the sound of his name.

"Hello Todd, how are you?"

"Ok, is it ok if I go up?"

"Yes, I don't see why not."

Ella could think of many reasons why she did not want Todd coming up to her bedroom. She sat up straighter, debating whether to get out of bed and head him off at the door but before she could decide, Todd was already there. He had an ugly smirk on his face as he looked down at her, recognising his position of power.

"I see you don't care who you have in your bedroom."

"Todd! What are you doing here?" Ella looked at the bunch of flowers he was holding.

Todd threw them to the side onto a chair. "They're not from me, Mum sent them."

"Well, what do you want? This isn't a good time." Ella fidgeted uneasily as Todd came closer, towering over the bed.

"I want my money back."

"We've already been through this."

"Yeah but I don't think my Mum would want you as a friend if she knew what you were up to. So, it's your choice. And it's my money not yours."

"We're not doing anything wrong Todd."

"No, but you haven't told her because - . Well, you don't want her to know do you?"

Ella's mobile phone rang on the bedside table, making her jump. She was pleased to see Todd jump too and gained a little courage from it. She picked it up and saw it was Libby calling again.

"It's your mother. I think you'd better leave Todd."

Todd was uneasy now and backed away a little. Had he gone too far? He looked at the flowers on the chair wondering if perhaps he should back-pedal a bit and offer to put them in the kitchen or apologise maybe, but he didn't do anything except run down the stairs and get out of Ella's cottage as quick as he could.

Ella, despite her early grogginess had insisted Libby tell Andrew to stay away. Partly she didn't want him to see her in this sorry state, but mostly she didn't want him to catch anything. Libby had given her an odd look, as if to question her assumption that Andrew would hot foot it over to mop her brow.

Andrew had phoned each evening and they agreed he should keep a low profile while Libby was playing head nurse, frequently popping in to check on Ella. The sound of his voice alone cheered her up and she couldn't wait to be up and about so that she could see him again.

Chapter Nineteen

The beginning of June and the garden looked beautiful. Libby sighed with contentment as she attempted to sit down on the old-fashioned traditional-style deck chair without spilling her tea in her lap. She was taking a well-deserved ten-minute break, enjoying the peace and quiet.

Admittedly she needed Mrs O'Brien and appreciated her help with the house but Libby was happy to take care of the garden entirely by herself. Sometimes, if she needed some extra muscle, she would get Todd to help. He didn't seem to mind, he even appeared to enjoy it. This morning she had been weeding and deadheading, sweeping the patio after the strong winds of the last few days and carrying out general maintenance.

Andrew was coming for lunch today. Libby had sent Todd and Jess along to Juliette's to choose a selection of cakes and to call for Andrew on their way back. They would be here any minute thought Libby as she attempted to lift herself out of the deck chair with some semblance of elegance. Failing that, but determined not to have to stay put until someone pulled her out, she wriggled forward until she was perched on the wooden cross bar and then stood up, vowing never to go near the thing again.

Libby laid a tablecloth on the large patio table, and brought the cushion pads from the shed for the chairs. Just as she was bringing out the cutlery and sauces, she heard voices from the lane and then Andrew appeared in the garden together with Todd and Jess who were each clutching a large cake box – enough cakes to last all week evidently. She knew it had been a mistake to send them out with a twenty-pound note, failing to mention a spending limit.

"Guess what?" said Jess, joining her mother in the kitchen, swinging the cake box gently, teasing.

"Oh, what?" Libby stopped what she was doing, curious.

"Juliette's had some of your favourite pineapple cheese-cake."

"Ooh did they now?" Pineapple cheesecake was Libby's all time favourite but Juliette's didn't always have it. "Did you get me one then?"

"No," said Jess, setting the box down carefully on the kitchen table. She turned to go back outside, stopping at the door and turning to smile at her mother. "I got you two! It is pineapple that's your favourite, isn't it?"

"Yes," laughed Libby at her teenage daughter's apparent relapse into a five year old.

"I thought so. Todd said it was blackcurrant but I knew it was pineapple." Libby popped her head around the door, half expecting to see Jess skipping up the garden. She didn't, but she smiled at the sight before her eyes anyway. Todd and Jess were laying the table with crockery, cutlery and napkins, side by side, no teasing or bickering. Andrew was sitting at the head of the table, looking relaxed and well, enjoying the summer sunshine. He looked good there, thought Libby. She liked it when Andrew was around. She enjoyed his company and well, just liked his presence. She hadn't seen that much of him lately. He must have been busy with various things because he had stopped popping by like he used to. It went like that sometimes and Libby would worry he was intentionally staying away as she was no longer married to his son. Perhaps he felt he had no right to call by when he wanted. But her worries were always unfounded and things eventually resumed back to normal, like today.

Perhaps she should make an effort to make Andrew feel more welcome, she thought. And then she had an idea. In fact, she had a doubly good idea.

"Andrew?"

"Mm?" Andrew slowly opened his eyes. The warmth from the sun was nearly sending him to sleep.

"How do you fancy coming over to dinner, say, next Saturday?"

"That'll be nice. Sounds a bit formal and forward planning. Are you plotting something?" Andrew was secretly hoping Libby was going to invite Ella along. He couldn't help himself, Libby was a lovely lady but the evening would be much more animated with Ella there.

"Actually, I am plotting something. I was thinking to invite Ella along –."

"Good idea," cut in Andrew, silently thanking his lucky stars.

"And….." Libby paused for effect. Andrew looked at Libby, questioning eyebrows raised. An excited Libby went and sat next to Andrew, eager to share her thoughts.

"Well, I thought of inviting Neil Cookson over as well. Make us a foursome. What do you think?"

"What do you want to invite him over for?" Andrew tried but failed to keep the irritation from his voice.

"Why do you think? I reckon they might get on well together. You know what I mean."

Andrew didn't like the idea of Libby trying to match-make for Ella, but he knew it wasn't right to make any claim on her.

"Well, go for it then. But they might not appreciate your interfering."

"It's not interfering!" Libby got up feeling a little put out at Andrew's telling off but also pleased he had agreed to come. "I'm just trying to help," she said as she went back inside, smiling.

Andrew walked along the beach, behind the huts as if he were going towards the esplanade and back along to his house. Libby had invited him to stay on for the evening but he had insisted he had sat still for too long and had eaten too much. He said he needed a walk and was worried for a second Libby would suggest joining him. He turned sharply now, at the last huts, walking around to the front to see the door open and Ella there waiting for him.

She beamed her now familiar smile as Andrew went up the steps and wrapped his arms around her. She loved the closeness of him, the feel of his strength around her. They went inside and Andrew sat down, Ella immediately snuggling in next to him, not wanting to waste a second of being close to him while she had the chance.

"I think we've been rumbled," said Andrew. Ella looked up into his face and was relieved to see the teasing smile that told her he wasn't being serious.

"By who?"

"Libby. Maybe. She wants to arrange a cosy foursome for a dinner party; me and Libby, and you and Neil Cookson. So, either she's onto us and is trying to do something about it or she genuinely thinks you and Neil will make a good couple."

Ella laughed. "I don't think she knows about us. She's just trying to be kind."

"You're probably right. I think if she knew, she'd have said something."

"Mm, but I don't think she'd like it, you know."

"No." They sat in silence for just a few moments.

"So, how do you feel about this Neil? He's quite good-looking isn't he?" Andrew got up and opened a bottle of red wine.

Ella didn't quite know what to make of it. "That's a bit of a strange question."

Andrew brushed it aside with one of his magic smiles which always made everything alright.

"Come on, shall we take this up?" he said grabbing two glasses and the bottle. Ella held the bottle while Andrew climbed the ladder and then she passed it up to him. She didn't really fancy anything to drink but it had become part of their ritual when they met at the hut, usually in the early evenings. It was their secret meeting place which made it all the more special to Ella. They would go back to their own homes under cover of darkness. All very clandestine and secret. They agreed it would be best for Andrew not to stay at Ella's cottage, much too close to Libby for comfort. And for some undisclosed reason they never stayed at Andrew's; it never came up in conversation. She hadn't even been to his house yet.

The wine tasted strange but she forced herself to drink some and then settled down in bed, where they made love and dozed and chatted long into the night.

Chapter Twenty

At last Libby had managed to get hold of Francine. She had been trying to arrange a time for them to meet up for days but Francine had not returned her calls. Libby had organised almost everything so far entirely on her own for the summer party. She had booked the marquee, caterers and bar, entertainment, and flower lady. Francine was notoriously difficult to contact so Libby had made most of the decisions off her own back. Actually, she was more than happy to take it all on. She knew how impressed Francine would be and consequently how grateful to her. Their friendship would be cemented forever.

Libby presumed it was the housekeeper who opened the door. She walked into the spacious, but not as grand as she expected, hallway where she was left alone for a few minutes. The housekeeper went off in one direction in search of Francine, muttering about how she wasn't sure where she was. An irate Francine emerged from the other direction, closely followed by her husband.

"Why can no-one ever do what they're told? When they're told to do it!"

"Calm down Fran, it'll sort itself out," said her softly spoken, completely unruffled husband. Francine was just about to launch into another barrage of fury when she spotted Libby. What was she doing here?

"Hello Libby? Oh, crikey, yes, I forgot." A few seconds of embarrassed silence followed. Libby was on the verge of suggesting she could come back another time but Roger saved the day.

"Libby, let's go through to the lounge. Francine will be with us in a few minutes." Without looking back at his wife, Roger led the way, graciously opening the door for her. Libby was grateful to be away from the prickly atmosphere but hoped Francine wasn't too put out by her being there.

A tray of tea and biscuits arrived and Libby watched Roger as he poured, offering milk and sugar. She had only met him briefly on a couple of occasions and had never noticed how very nice he was. Libby tittered on the inside at the inaccuracy of describing this man as 'nice'. Handsome, extremely good-looking – absolutely gorgeous in fact. No wonder Francine followed him in his tracks on his work related globetrotting, she'd be mad not to.

Far from appearing awkward that he had been landed the job of babysitting his wife's friend whom he didn't even know, Roger was completely at ease, making Libby feel totally looked after and relaxed in his company. They chatted easily for some time, discovering a common fondness for solitary dog walking and a love of living by the sea. Libby hadn't had a single thought of summer parties, marquees, flowers or food.

Francine entered the room and Libby was aware of the immediate change in atmosphere. She actually felt disappointed that Francine hadn't stayed away longer. Her disappointment increased as Roger got up. "I'll leave you ladies to it then. I know when I'm not wanted." Libby noticed how Francine didn't even acknowledge him leaving and watched him cross the room; right up to the second he disappeared through the doorway. Finally, she turned back to face Francine who was giving her an impatient look. Libby swallowed hard, a little embarrassed and not entirely sure she hadn't been sitting there with her mouth open.

"Shall we get down to business?" said Francine. "I don't have an awful lot of time I'm afraid," she said, checking her watch.

"Yes, we should, we've only got a few weeks to go."

Libby focused her thoughts on the matters in hand. A new excitement in the summer party had revived her previously flagging enthusiasm and she flicked through the pages of her folder running speedily down the list of things she needed to run by Francine; the colour scheme for the flowers and balloons, the costing for the children's entertainment - a futuristic puppet show, and the timetable for who would be arriving when on the days leading up to the 20th August.

Francine seemed distracted. She got up from the sofa and paced up and down along the wall which had three sets of French doors leading out onto the garden and grounds beyond. She simply nodded in agreement to most things and told Libby to do whatever she thought best for the rest.

Libby looked across to where Francine was standing with her back to her. She noticed how without her expensive, well-cut tailoring draped over her, she looked quite gangly.

Francine turned and once again glared at her watch. "I'm afraid I have to go Libby. Sorry to cut this so short but I have a prior appointment."

"But we still have a lot of things to go through on the list."

"Well, you just do what you think best." She broke into a smile which Libby noticed was the first one she'd seen from her all afternoon. "And anyway, it sounds like you've got everything all under control. You're doing a fantastic job." Her words of encouragement did the trick.

Libby beamed with pride. She was coming to the conclusion Francine wasn't really the slightest bit interested in being involved in the nitty-gritty of the party. She just wanted a good job done. And Libby was more than happy to be the one to do it. It would all be worth the effort once Francine saw for herself what she was capable of.

Chapter Twenty-One

Ella slowly lowered the novel onto the bed, in a semi-state of shock. She'd been tired again, like she was most afternoons lately and had come upstairs for a nap. She was halfway through the book beside her and hadn't been able to resist delving in for a few pages, despite feeling so tired.

The main character, a single woman in her early forties, was enjoying a reckless fling with her Spanish teacher. She'd been feeling unwell and on page ninety-six it suddenly dawned on her that she could be pregnant.

Ella let the book close without putting the marker in place. She sat bolt upright, her heart pounding, with absolute certainty. She hadn't felt right ever since the time around the fever and chest infection she'd had just after her birthday and had just put it down to a slow recovery from that. Ella stood and went over to the window, her legs feeling shaky and wobbly beneath her. She looked out to the sea beyond trying to take in the enormity of what she was thinking. Of what might be happening.

Her head was swimming with thoughts from every direction. Andrew, and what he would say, what would the future hold for them, was there really a 'them' to have a future together? She tried to think back and calculate properly but her mind was going crazy and she couldn't order her thoughts. She must get a proper test and find out for sure.

And if it was really true - but she couldn't dare let herself think that far ahead. Well, maybe just a sneaky peek; could it be possible that she would really have her own child? Ella could feel tears well in her eyes but she stopped herself, blinking them away and swallowing hard.

She made a decision to not indulge in any more of these happy thoughts until she knew for sure. She turned back to the bed, needing to do something practical, picking up the book and placing it neatly and precisely on the bedside table and then smoothed the bed cover. Everything was in slow motion. It was as though all her senses had been brought into a much sharper focus; the feel of the book, the silence of the room, even the colours of the bedspread seemed more vibrant. She picked up the book again and flicked through the pages to the bit that had struck a nerve with her like a lightening bolt. Ella read it again but, of course, it didn't have the same effect but she read it over a few times anyway, enjoying the sensation of that first realisation.

Ella tried to think clearly about what she should do next. She decided not to go to her local chemist to buy a pregnancy testing kit – Mrs Kelly seemed to know everyone and wasn't exactly discreet. Ella decided to go to the larger supermarket a little way out. She might just possibly bump into someone she knew there but with a trolley full of provisions, it would be easy to hide a little box amongst them.

First she needed to change out of her comfy, sloppy dress which was loose and baggy and which she now realised she had lived in for the last couple of weeks. Ella took her jeans from the back of the chair and wriggled into them, catching the reflection of herself in the full length mirror as she smiled a little smile of satisfaction at their very definite tightness. She couldn't resist standing sideways and checking her profile but there was no noticeable difference to see.

Ella spent ages wandering around the supermarket, pushing the trolley like she did every week but today particularly noticing the little child seat at the front. It seemed as though every other trolley in the supermarket had a child seat occupied with a little passenger or two.

She ambled along, leisurely choosing her items and gradually making her way towards the pharmaceutical area. As soon as she got there, she scanned the shelves for the type of product she was after and picked up the first appropriate-looking box and threw it into her trolley, looking surreptitiously about her as though she'd just stashed something in her handbag.

She felt flustered and hot and ready to leave. She twirled her trolley around to the opposite direction and sped towards the checkouts. At the end of the aisle, she almost ran a man down. It was only a neat side step on his part that saved him from having a trolley jammed into his thigh. A jar of baby food fell from his heavily over-laden basket. It rolled across the floor, stopping at Ella's right foot. She picked it up and handed it back to the man, raising her eyebrows questioningly as she saw that it was Neil Cookson. She looked at him, then at the jar of baby food then back at him again. "You have children?"

"No, no." Ho looked a little embarrassed and had a silly smirk on his face, his mouth firmly closed. An expression which said defiantly that he wasn't going to say anything more.

"You just prefer baby food to grown-up dinner party food." Ella was teasing him for not turning up to Libby's cosy dinner for four. Libby had been disappointed; Andrew and herself were simply relieved. She wondered if Neil had suspected he'd been set up. She was amused at his unimaginative excuse of a last minute medical emergency although, of course, it might have been true.

Ella pushed her trolley to a vacant checkout and started to unload, to-ing and fro-ing from the trolley to pack some bags. Just as she was about to return to the trolley to unload some more, she saw that Neil Cookson was right behind her in the queue.

"Shall I unload, while you pack?" he asked pleasantly.

"No! Thank-you, no, I'll be fine," said Ella, tugging her trolley possessively towards her.

Something fell to the floor. A small item had slipped through the bars of the trolley. The doctor bent down to retrieve it and handed Ella the pregnancy testing kit, with raised questioning eyebrows. Ella simply took the box, keeping her mouth firmly shut with a look she hoped said 'I'm not saying anything'. And also 'mind your own business and don't forget you're a doctor and should respect people's privacy.'

Ella had never packed shopping as quickly as she did that afternoon. She then got confused with her money, thinking she had enough to pay with cash. Embarrassed, she fumbled for a card to pay with and then keyed in the wrong pin number. Finally finished, with her trolley laden, she virtually ran out of the shop to the car park.

A short while later, while unpacking and putting away her shopping, she laughed at herself, embarrassed now at how silly she'd been just because Neil Cookson had seen her buying a pregnancy test kit. Yes, I bet he was really shocked at that, thought Ella highly amused. A thirty-seven year old woman getting pregnant – I bet there weren't many scandals like that in this village. Ella picked up the box from the kitchen worktop and mentally corrected herself, a thirty-seven year old woman *suspecting* she was pregnant. She took her time unpacking the rest of the shopping, fiddling with the little box every now and then, aware she was procrastinating, avoiding the result and the enormity of what it would mean. In the last few hours her life had potentially changed in a way she didn't even dare dream of anymore.

Ella was bent double, sitting on the edge of the bed, tears streaming down her face. She couldn't stop shaking and even felt slightly sick. She wanted to scream with happiness and was feeling the urge to jump up and down on the bed. Instead she simply lay back, staring at the ceiling relishing the joy of the moment. She laid there for some time and then realised with some amusement how hungry she was.

Tucking into a sandwich, Ella turned her attention to the next immediate job in hand which was to tell Andrew. She was aware it was still early days and she had no intention of shouting her news from the rooftops but Andrew, of all people, should be told.

She had to find the piece of paper with his home phone number on it. She hardly ever phoned him, the usual thing was for him to phone her. After she'd dialled the number, it rang for some time before he answered and he sounded surprised to hear her voice.

"I thought I might pop round and see you." There was a fraction of a pause which Ella felt she had to fill. "I have something to tell you." She hoped he would pick up on the excitement in her voice.

"Well actually, I have a couple of friends around at the moment." Now it was Ella's turn to pause. She certainly didn't want to make her announcement in front of an audience but for some reason she'd imagined Andrew would be alone.

"Can it wait until tomorrow?" Andrew asked. "I was going to ring you in the morning anyway and suggest lunch. We haven't been to The Tea Cosy for ages." His voice was soothing, relaxed and gentle, as always. "Do you fancy that?"

"Yes, ok, that'll be lovely. I'll see you tomorrow then."

Ella put down the phone, a little bemused at their rather odd conversation. Despite this, she was still smiling. She didn't think she would be able to stop even if she wanted to. She went out into the garden, the grass cold under her bare feet and with hands on hips she inhaled deeply, imagining the clean, fresh air circulating throughout her body, feeding oxygen to all its vital organs and of course to another tiny set of organs just forming and hopefully growing healthily. With a sense of satisfaction, she was happier than ever to be living in this part of the world, next to the sea and the beach – natural and healthy.

Ella couldn't help but wonder if it was psychological but whether it was or not, this morning she felt sick. Gut wrenching sick. The thought of food made her even queasier but she managed to drink a cup of tea although she didn't risk having another two or three cups like she did most mornings. She had woken early and had laid there for a while going over the miraculous and momentous happenings of yesterday but had felt so nauseous, she had to get up.

Now, she was washed and dressed and just about feeling normal but was disappointed Andrew still hadn't phoned. There was no way she could sit still long enough let alone concentrate on doing any work and so she made a snap decision to go to his house to tell him the news. Perhaps she would have an appetite by then and they could enjoy a celebratory breakfast together.

As she walked along the lane, she wondered seriously what Andrew's reaction would be. Realising she'd been so caught up in her own elation she hadn't considered for a moment that the father of this baby might not feel the same. Ella slowed down a little and then stopped to take a rest on a stone wall. Andrew already had two children and it suddenly dawned on her he might not be too happy at having another, which led her onto another train of thought, a question which Andrew might be keen to know the answer to - how had this happened? What if he thought she had been using him just to get what she'd wanted? She tried to reason with herself. They had both been there and both knew what they were doing and neither of them had questioned anything. She felt a little stupid and also slightly awkward although nothing was going to diminish her happiness at what had happened as a result.

Ella continued on her way, a little less enthusiastically now. She wished Andrew would simply take one look at her and telepathically pick up on everything she'd been through in the last twenty-four hours to save her from what now seemed an effort to try to explain.

Andrew came to the door and Ella thought she saw the tiniest flicker of irritation as he opened it to see her standing there. If it was there at all, it was gone in an instant.

"Hello. You must be very hungry for lunch then." Andrew kissed her gently on her forehead as she stepped into the hallway. She went automatically into the room on the right which looked like the lounge-come-study while Andrew went into the kitchen, calling out to her to see if she wanted tea or coffee. She looked around her. Here was an insight into Andrew and his world that she was seeing for the first time. They spent most of their time together in the beach hut.

The room was filled with clutter, piles and piles of books, mostly art books and small canvases dotted all over the room in different stages of completion. She couldn't believe it of herself but she had actually forgotten Andrew painted. He liked to paint portraits, she did remember him telling her that. And here she was looking at all these different faces but she didn't know any of them. And yet she also remembered Andrew saying he only liked to paint people he knew so he could attempt to bring out their particular quirk or characteristic.

The room was dark, despite the large window to the front of the house which overlooked the garden. It was more to do with the large furniture and the amount of it crammed into the room; the shelves of books, the large desk under the window and the dark almost foreboding furnishings in green velvet. It was a very masculine room, a very single man's room, Ella concluded. She'd only been here a few minutes but in that time had learnt much about its occupant. The most significant thing being, whatever Ella was to Andrew, she was only one very small part of his very busy, fully occupied life. And from the feeling she got from his home, the settled stability and permanent way of life, she was quite convinced he didn't want it to change.

Andrew appeared with two mugs of tea and set them down on the brown leather coasters on the low coffee table. As he sat down on the settee, Ella noticed he must have been painting when she called. A half finished picture on the desk, a palette of mixed paints and a single fine paintbrush placed to one side made her grimace to think she had disturbed him.

He looked over at Ella and smiled his easy, warm smile. Ella was aware the expression on her face was far from easy and warm but she couldn't help it. She felt tense and anxious.

"Come and sit down, you look worn out. Yes, you were going to tell me something."

"I just called by to say I'm sorry but I won't be able to make it for lunch today. I've got an urgent article to do, it's just come up, all very last minute, bit of a pain really." Ella was flapping her arms about, trying to be as convincing as possible.

"That's ok," said Andrew reassuringly. He took a sip of his tea and leant back, stretching his long legs in front of him. A clocked ticked loudly. Ella didn't know what to do with herself. For some reason she didn't want to go across the room and sit with Andrew. She stayed where she was leaning against the desk. Andrew grinned at her and she gave a little smile back, studying his expression as if looking at a painting for the first time, her head cocked to one side in concentration. His grin was that of a slightly wicked cheeky child but also incredibly sexy and enticing at the same time, all very beguiling in a man of his age and experience. For a second, Ella felt completely out of her depth. What was she doing here?

"Come on, you were going to tell me something. You sounded quite excited last night. You've gone all quiet on me."

Ella relaxed a little at last, seeing again the Andrew she'd fallen for, easy and intuitive, safe and warm. Just today, a little unreachable. She went and sat next to him but kept a little distance between them as she picked up her mug of tea.

"Well, it seems a bit silly now, but all it is is that I'm having Colette here to stay with me for a while, my step-daughter. Remember, I've mentioned her before?"

"Yes, yes, of course I remember. That sounds like a nice idea."

He didn't say anymore on the subject, Ella noticed. He didn't express an interest to meet Colette or suggest they should all get together, and Ella suspected that from now on she would probably make many more such observations.

Ella headed back home, taking the longer route via the beach. She couldn't stop thinking about Andrew, so complete in his own world. She just couldn't bring herself, in that moment, to shatter the solid stability he had created for himself. She ambled along the beach, feeling confused and deflated. She wanted to share her news with someone, see and hear them excited for her. But then she reprimanded herself for getting carried away. It was still very early days for her. She decided to phone Colette that evening and see if she was ready yet to make a visit.

Ella arrived at her beach hut and sat down for a rest on the bottom step, slipping off her sandals and burrowing her feet into the warm sand. She gazed along the beach and saw in the distance, a man out for a jog. He was heading in her direction and as he came closer, she recognised it was Neil Cookson. He raised his hand in recognition, slowed down and eventually stopped in front of her, a little out of breath.

"Hi," he said, bending over, resting his hands on his knees.

"Hello," Ella smiled.

"I'm in training. Hoping to do the London marathon next year."

"You're going to have to do more training," she said cheekily, noticing his red face and heavy breathing.

"Well, thank-you for your observation. I am monitoring myself, I'll have you know and I'm getting there. Plenty of time yet. And speaking of monitoring, I take it you'll be coming to see me soon?"

Ella stood up to go, surprised at his directness. "I suppose I will." She picked up her sandals, and strolled passed Neil Cookson. "I hope you enjoyed the baby food?"

"Of course. I always do. Banana's my favourite flavour."

Secateurs in hand, Libby peered over the hedge towards Ella's cottage. Out of the corner of her eye she saw Jess come into the garden and immediately resumed her hedge-trimming pose. She turned to see Jess spreading a bath towel onto the lawn and settle herself for a sunbathing session. Libby was pleased she'd got away with it. She hated it when her daughter chided her for being a nosey neighbour but lately, Libby had been at it constantly. Something was going on and Libby suspected she knew exactly what it was.

Dr Cookson was making another call on Ella. His car was there on her drive for all to see. The question was, was it a personal call or a professional one, or maybe both. Libby smiled to herself knowingly.

Ella hadn't seen much of Neil Cookson lately. She had registered at the local surgery as his patient but her one check up and scan so far had been at the hospital. It was nice to see him today. He'd come to return her sailing book and had stayed for a quick cup of tea and a chat.

Libby wished Ella would tell her in person; after all they were good friends. But she had decided she would say nothing. She would wait until Ella was ready to confide in her. After all, Libby was the mother of two, and she knew the signs.

There was still no sign of Neil Cookson coming out of Ella's cottage and Libby was fed up with pretending to trim the hedge. She was suddenly tempted to pop over to her neighbour under pretence of needing to borrow something or other but thought maybe that was taking the whole prying thing a little too far.

"Mum?"

Libby jumped. "Yes? What?" she said defensively.

"Just wondered if you were making a cup of tea?" she said cheekily, propping herself up on her elbows and grinning at her mum.

"Mm, you're in luck. I was just about to go in and make a cup." As she entered the house, Libby heard the familiar low roar of a sports car go passed.

"Damn!" If she'd stayed on mock hedge duty for just a bit longer, she might have glimpsed a good-bye kiss. Just something conclusively corroborative to satisfy her, that her matchmaking plan had been a success.

Chapter Twenty-Two

Ella had been commissioned to write a series of articles on small businesses on the south east coast and how they were being affected by the current economy.

She had set up her desk in the small bedroom but it was chilly and draughty up there even in July and although it had a pretty view of the village and its church, she much preferred looking out over the sea. Plus, the previous tenant's hideous taste in décor didn't help. Bright orange walls with brown painted woodwork did nothing to help her concentration. The room, all being well, was the one she intended to use for the baby and when she'd started daydreaming of replacing the horrid orange with some soft pastel colour and making lists of all her other plans for the room, she knew it was time to move herself elsewhere in the house, otherwise she would never get any work done.

Now comfortably settled at the kitchen table, she still couldn't focus. With her pen hovering above the blank sheet of paper glaring up at her, she decided to make a cup of tea. It was ten o'clock – time for a break even if she hadn't actually done anything yet. She was trying to finish an article about a family-run boat building business and needed to interview the owner. She could do it over the phone; it would be quicker and more convenient for both of them but she hadn't been able to get hold of him and was waiting for him to call her back. She was a bit stuck until she got the information she needed.

Ella took her mug of tea and stood in front of the window looking across her pretty garden to the beach below. It was a beautiful day, perfect clear blue skies and warm sunshine. It was lovely to see people out and about in their short sleeves. Ella hoped it would be a long summer although she didn't know how she would be able to resist spending all her time down there on the beach. It was difficult enough today to find the discipline to stay indoors and work.

There was, of course, one thing helping her to focus and that was the thought that in a few months she was hoping to take some time off to completely dedicate herself to her new baby son or daughter. She knew she should work solidly until then, take on as much as she could to put some extra savings away. She had already acknowledged how lucky she was to be able to work from home. There would be no need for a child minder; it would be fantastic. She'd be able to go back to work as soon as she liked; working hours to suit herself. It felt like a dream.

Completely carried away by her daydream, the sound of the phone made her jump. She put her mug down on the table, grabbed her notebook and pen before answering the phone in her efficient business voice.

"Hello, Ella Peters."

"Hello Ella." She recognised the voice immediately. "It's Jon."

"I know, I mean yes, hello." There was a pause. Ella was waiting for Jon to speak but for some reason he was hesitating, waiting for her to say something. But she couldn't think of anything.

"How are you Ella?"

"I'm very well, actually, thank-you."

"Good. You sound good." Jon sounded tired, absolutely worn out, in fact, but Ella didn't want to hear his troubles about how hard it was having a new baby around. He'd made his bed.

"The reason I'm phoning - is Colette with you yet? She was driving up to see you."

"No, she's not with me. I've not even spoken to her for a while. Why do you think she's here?"

"We were talking last night and she got upset, said she was off to stay with you for a couple of days."

"What about Simon? They haven't split up have they?"

"No, no they're fine. He's away on business, coming back in the next couple of days. She didn't want to be on her own. That's why she wanted to come to you." There was another pause. Jon sounded out of breath. It was a good few seconds before he began again.

"She just took off and drove through the night. But I haven't heard from her since. She should have been there hours ago. Oh Christ!"

"Wait a minute, Jon, just hang on a second. If she's here already and she probably is, I know where she'll be." It was as if they'd never been apart, slipping back into their easy ways. When one of them was stressed or worried, the other would automatically take the lead. "Give me a little while, I'll go and look, and give you a call back, ok?"

"Thanks Ella."

Ella put the phone down and stared at it, contemplating what had just happened. Her previous instinct would have been to analyse the conversation, to dissect it and look for a hidden message but she didn't feel the need. She didn't really feel anything. And then, like a slap in the face, she remembered the purpose of the call - Colette.

Ella ran down the steps to the beach as fast as she could but running across the sand soon became hard work and remembering her precious cargo, she slowed to a more gentle jog towards the beach huts. From a distance, the hut looked undisturbed but as Ella got closer and then mounted the wooden steps, she saw the padlock was missing.

She turned the handle slowly, not wanting to frighten the person inside and fully expected the inner bolt to be securely in place but was surprised when the door opened. It was dark inside with the curtains still pulled. There was just a hint of light coming from the tiny window up in the rafters. Someone was moving around up there. Ella squinted as her eyes adjusted to the darkness. Suddenly a head peeked out from a shroud of blankets, eyes wide, as if caught out. "Who's there? Ella, is that you? It's me Colette. Thank god you're here."

Even from down on the ground, Ella could see Colette was distraught. She was already making her way down the ladder, her skirt and jumper creased from where she'd obviously slept in her clothes. Colette was in a state. She climbed down the ladder in such a hurry she slipped and nearly lost her footing completely. At the bottom and on firm ground she looked at Ella who walked slowly towards her, taking in the look of desperation on her tired and weary face. Something had happened, something of such magnitude Colette obviously didn't know where to start and equally Ella was too scared to prompt her, preferring a few more seconds of safe silence.

Ella held out her arms and Colette fell against her. Ella held her tight expecting to feel her sobs which would inevitably come even though the reason for them was not yet apparent. But Colette simple rested against her, totally spent. Finally she pulled back, and sat down, still not speaking a word.

Ella sat next to her and took her hands in hers.

"Colette?" Colette just stared straight ahead. "When did you get here? And why didn't you come up to the cottage?" Ella spoke as gently as she possibly could.

"I did. But I didn't want to wake you. So I came here."

"What time was that?"

"I don't know. It was just getting light."

"You drove through the night?"

Colette nodded. "I had to get away. Get away from everything. You don't mind do you? That I came here?"

"No, of course I don't mind. I'm glad you're here. But Colette, you're going to have to tell me, what this is all about. Your Dad's been on the phone, he's worried about you."

Ella sobbed into her hands. "Dad. Oh god! My poor Dad."

Ella sat in silence, waiting patiently.

"He's not well. He's really ill," whispered Colette in between sobs.

Ella didn't respond immediately and the simple statement was left hanging in the air – the enormity of its implications apparent to both of them.

"What's wrong exactly?"

"Some kind of blood disease. What does it matter?"

"What treatment is he having? You mustn't lose hope –."

Colette cut in bluntly. "Nothing. There's nothing they can do. They've already said that."

"Oh Colette. I don't know what to say." Ella leant in close, holding Colette's hands tighter. She looked down at their mingled fingers and noticed for the first time, the engagement ring.

"You're engaged."

For a fraction of a second Ella felt a little put out because she hadn't been told about this special event. But looking into Colette's eyes, no explanation was necessary, it was immediately clear why Colette and Simon had suddenly decided to get engaged.

Through her tears, Colette managed to mumble, "I'm sorry you didn't know. We only did it a few days ago."

"I understand Colette. It's ok. Really, it's all ok. Come on, let's get up to the cottage."

Colette stood and started to gather her few things together, she moved wearily, mechanically, all the time tears trickled down her face which she appeared oblivious to as if she were just so used to them being there. Colette blinked hard to adjust to the bright sunshine outside. "I'm sorry about your padlock. I had to smash it off. My key didn't fit and I didn't know what else to do. I'll buy you another one."

"Don't worry about it," said Ella as she secured the door with a piece of string she'd grabbed on her way out, remembering the last time someone had smashed the lock off – it had been Andrew on her birthday. It seemed like ages ago already. She and Colette certainly had a lot to talk about.

Inside the cottage, Colette had at last stopped crying although her eyes still looked red and sore. Her skin was blotchy and raw from her salty tears and the attempts to wipe them away. She stood in the middle of the kitchen like a lost child waiting to be told what to do.

"Take a seat," said Ella as she quickly cleared the table of her work things and put the kettle on. An ugly thought was emerging which she was trying not to acknowledge. She was wishing Colette would go away and take all this horribleness with her. She was afraid to find out more information and at the same time she wanted to know every detail of Jon's illness, just as she would if she were still his wife, and then she would want to find out what they could do to help him, because she would never lose hope. There must be something they could do. He was newly married and had a baby daughter, for goodness sake, he had everything to live for.

They drank their tea in silence. Ella thought to offer breakfast but the idea of food made her feel sick and so she said nothing. It seemed neither of them wanted to talk.

"Do you want to phone your Dad, let him know you're ok?"

Colette shook her head. Ella didn't feel like speaking to him either, so she took the coward's way and sent him a text message, saying Colette would phone him later.

"Are you ok?" asked Ella.

"Just tired, really, really tired."

Ella took her up to the spare bedroom, all newly decorated in pink and white, still looking fresh and clean and pretty. But neither of them made a comment on it. Colette lay down on top of the bed and Ella covered her in a pink throw, more for comfort than warmth. It was still a blue skies and bright sunshine day outside, deceptively happy, thought Ella as she pulled the curtains across in an attempt to dim the brightness in the room and in doing so discovered the pale pink, unlined curtains weren't much use for that. She turned back to Colette to see if there was anything else she needed but she had her eyes closed and judging by her calm, deep breathing, was already asleep.

Back downstairs, Ella felt tired herself but knew her mind was way too busy to let her settle for a nap. She made herself another cup of tea and sat in the armchair in the kitchen looking out the window to sea, trying to make sense of the bits and pieces of information she'd got from Colette that morning.

She gathered the latest diagnosis had been made fairly recently which explained the rush engagement. Colette had told her that her father was back in hospital for a few days but she hadn't said why. Through her tears, she had mumbled something about wanting to run away from everything and how she couldn't bear the thought of having to spend time with Danielle who - what had Colette said? Ella tried to remember her exact words. She had said, "She didn't give a stuff about anyone but herself." Surely, Jon had the support and care of his wife. After all, they had only been married a few months. Although, in all fairness, she must be struggling with everything at the moment - Jon being ill and a young baby to look after.

Ella's head was pounding. She massaged her left temple in small circular movements, knowing she wouldn't even consider taking something for a headache. She closed her eyes and managed to doze restlessly on and off for an hour or so.

It was mid afternoon before Colette came downstairs. Ella woke as she heard her descend the creaky stairs.

"Sorry, I didn't mean to wake you."

"It's ok, I was only dozing. Do you feel better for your sleep?"

"Yes, much better. Shall I make more tea?" Colette smiled.

"Yes, more tea. That always helps." They laughed.

"Shall I make us a sandwich as well? I'm a little hungry."

"Good idea. If you don't mind, that'll be lovely. I'm not much of a hostess, am I? Getting you to make your own food."

"I wasn't exactly invited was I?" Colette had noticed how Ella looked tired too and understood that even though they were divorced, she would still worry about her Dad.

Ella settled back into the armchair. She would find the energy later to cook a nice meal for Colette but at the moment, she was happy just to sit there for a while and let Colette take over. She smiled as she heard her banging around in the kitchen, making tea and putting the washed dishes away. It was nice having her around even under such unhappy circumstances.

They ate their late lunch then went for a walk along the beach. It was still pleasantly warm and they strolled along, stopping occasionally to pick up a shell or a particularly perfect pebble, comparing each other's finds. They reached the beach hut and took a breather on the steps for a while, sitting side by side in silence, staring out to sea and infinity beyond.

They had a stroll around the shops, looking in the windows and making trivial comments about the tacky souvenirs in the gift shops and faking interest in the shoes and bags in the more expensive boutiques. A little café caught their attention more because it was quiet and empty than anything else. It was plain and rather dull inside but reassuringly clean. It smelled of fish and chips which reminded them both of family holidays and happy times which in turn made them want to cry. They sat at a table close to the window, ordered cappuccinos and chocolate brownies and ate in silence as they looked out the window at all the busy people getting on with their lives. Colette studied their faces to see if she could identify anyone else who had a father who was ill, she was sure she would be able to tell. Ella thought it incredible how the whole world and their mother seemed to be pregnant. She nearly made a comment to this effect but managed to stop herself. There would be plenty of time for that later.

Their final stop was the little supermarket where Ella shopped for their dinner, trying to think on the spot of something she could do which wouldn't keep her in the kitchen all evening. She bought a free range chicken to roast and lots of fresh salad and a couple of bottles of wine, one being non-alcoholic which she hoped would escape Colette's attention.

"What's with this non-alcoholic stuff?" said Colette as she took a bottle of chilled wine from the fridge while Ella basted the chicken. "You trying to be good?"

"Well, I'm trying to cut down, you know."

"Mm, do you mind if I open the other one? We can have this one later, maybe, if we're desperate."

"Well, I'll have one of the non-alco ones. You start on the other bottle."

They ate their dinner in the kitchen, scraped their plates and then piled them next to the sink to deal with later. They took their wine into the living room which was chilly despite it still being light and sunny outside. The sun never shone directly into the room and it never seemed to really warm up. They sat next to each other on the settee, time to talk, at last.

"What are your plans Colette? And before you answer, you know you can stay here as long as you want to."

"Thanks Ella. It's ok; Dad's supposed to be coming out of hospital the day after tomorrow. And Simon's home then too. So I'll go back then. I hope you don't mind me coming here. I didn't want to stay in the flat on my own – not at the moment, with all this swimming around in my head."

"It's absolutely fine, really."

"And there's no way I'm staying in Dad's house, with that woman."

Ella smiled a little, she wasn't sure how much of Colette's dislike for Danielle was purely for her sake.

"What's he in for, is he having some treatment?"

"No, a few more tests, to see if he is suitable for any treatment."

"Well, that's hopeful, isn't it?"

Colette nodded feebly.

"And what will you do, go straight to the hospital? I take it Danielle's picking him up?"

Colette gave a snort, a look of disdain on her face. "Who knows?"

Ella inclined her head, not understanding.

"Danielle is a total nightmare," she said categorically.

Ella couldn't hide her surprise. Colette looked just a little shame-faced as she spoke but carried on anyway. "She's the worst decision Dad ever made," she said quietly. "And they argue all the time."

Again Ella was surprised. Neither she nor Jon was the arguing type. But then again, she didn't think Jon was the leaving his wife and going off with a younger woman type either. And she never regarded herself as the type who got pregnant by a much older man whom she'd only known for a few months. Who was to judge?

Colette amended her statement. "She's always sounding off, making a right fuss about something or other. Dad just puts up with all the ranting and then finally he gets to where he's had enough and gives it all right back." Colette gave a little laugh. "And she can't stand me which is fine because the feeling's mutual."

Ella sighed, still tired and now weary with an overwhelming feeling of hopelessness about everything. She felt her eyes start to water and could feel that her face was red.

"Ella, are you ok? Oh god, I didn't mean to upset you."

"It's ok, I'm fine. Sorry, I just think it's so sad."

They sat in silence for a couple of seconds, and then Colette continued. "That's not the worst thing. She drinks a lot. Too much I think. And then she goes off on one." Colette was staring at the floor, speaking barely above a whisper. "And worst of all, she strops out of the house and goes racing off in her car – sometimes taking Isobel with her, drives my Dad half crazy with worry." Ella was speechless finding it difficult to believe what she had just heard.

"Aren't you worried about them, well, about Isobel? Leaving her with just Danielle?"

"I would be. No, it's ok, Danielle's sister's staying there for a while. She's ok actually, only nineteen and completely the opposite to Danielle and she loves Isobel to bits. I'm not sure she likes Danielle much actually, which is a big plus."

"Oh Colette, I had no idea things were so bad."

"Why should you? It's not your problem! I'm sorry Ella, I didn't mean it to sound like that – it's just, you know, none of this should really be your concern. It's not fair, I shouldn't have come here."

"Enough of that rubbish. You can come here whenever you want and talk to me about anything you want. Ok? And we can sit up and talk half the night if you want to. Now finish that glass of wine and I'll fill it up. And any more nonsense and I'll give you the yucky non-alcoholic stuff."

They did talk into the night and into the early hours too. Colette seemed to suddenly run out of steam and Ella sent her off to bed while she made herself a cup of hot milk. Her stomach turned at the smell of stale food coming from the pile of dirty dishes but she wasn't about to tackle them now, they would have to wait until the morning. She noticed the papers and notes on the side for her half written article and resolved to make finishing it an absolute priority once Colette had gone back to London.

Ella took her mug of milk up to bed and reflected on the evening's conversation. She was shocked to learn of the desperately unhappy situation Jon seemed to be in. This last year for him had resulted in complete turmoil. And for her too, she reminded herself. She finished her milk, switched off the bedside light and lay down with such a busy mind, she knew she would hardly be able to sleep.

It was light when Ella woke but instinctively she knew she'd only been asleep for a short while and that it wasn't the alarm clock that had woken her. She looked across, three-thirty and then she heard the phone ringing. She hurried down the stairs but it must have been ringing for a while already as it stopped just before she picked up. Punching in the code to find out the number of the person who'd called, she recognised it immediately as Jon's but despite continuous attempts to reach him, his number was engaged. She paused for a few seconds and jumped when the phone rang.

"Hello Jon?"

"No, it's Simon."

"Oh hello Simon. That's weird, Jon was just trying to call." Ella was still groggy with sleep and couldn't make sense of what was happening. Colette was suddenly at her side, anxious to know what was going on.

"You've not spoken to Jon yet?" asked Simon.

"No. What's going on Simon? Is he ok?"

"Not really no. Oh god, is Colette there? I don't really know who to talk to."

"Yes, she's here. Shall I put her on?"

"No. It'll be better if you tell her, I think. Oh Christ, Ella." Simon took a deep breath. "There's been an accident. Danielle, she's been in a car accident."

"Oh my god."

Colette grabbed Ella's arm, anxious to know what on earth had happened.

"Is she, is she badly injured?" Ella was thinking the worst but couldn't bring herself to put it into words. Simon confirmed it for her.

"Ella she's dead."

"Oh my god." Ella put her arm around Colette, as much to steady herself as to provide comfort. "What about the baby? Oh please say the baby's ok."

"Yes, she's ok, she wasn't in the car. It was just Danielle and another woman, a friend they think. She's badly injured but alive. Danielle was driving and took the worst of it – no other cars involved. Is Colette there with you?"

"Yes she is. I need to explain this to her. How's Jon doing?"

"Not great. He tried ringing you but then asked me to do it. If Colette wants to be with her Dad –."

"She will do," cut in Ella; certain Colette would want to leave as soon as possible.

"Well, Jon asked me to come down for her, he's worried about her driving alone."

"Yes, of course. When will you be able to get here?"

"I can be there in a couple of hours."

"Ok, we'll see you then."

Ella replaced the phone, turned to Colette and held her hand.

"It's Danielle, isn't it?"

"Yes, a car accident."

"And she's dead isn't she?" Colette gripped her stomach as if she were about to be sick. She hurried into the living room and plonked herself down before her shaky legs gave way. Ella sat beside her rubbing her back. There were no tears from either of them, only silent shock.

Ella filled the kettle, she'd pushed the tap on too hard and water spurted everywhere. She had an urge to hit something – hard. The sight of the dirty dishes was infuriating and she filled the sink with hot soapy water and piled them in so violently, she was sure half of them would be chipped - but she didn't care.

Ella and Colette sipped their tea. It occurred to Ella that only a few hours ago they had been sitting in exactly the same place, sipping wine and chatting and in the short time since then people's lives had been destroyed forever.

"I said some terrible things about her last night," said Colette.

"Mm, I've said some pretty awful things about her too over the past year."

"I've hated her, really hated her."

"Colette stop. I've wished her dead. How terrible is that? But I didn't really mean it, I suppose. You mustn't feel guilty for having bad thoughts. This is a terrible thing yes, but it's one of those things. It's nobody's fault." Ella sounded more generous than she felt. She was wrestling with her own guilty conscious, remembering the prolonged hostility she'd felt towards Jon and his young wife.

"It's your Dad you need to think about. He's going to need you desperately." Ella was tired and it was an effort to speak but the silence was worse. She got up and pulled the curtains to let in the sunshine and hopefully some warmth into the cold room. They sat for a while longer sipping lukewarm tea and then Colette went back upstairs to dress and collect her few things together.

Simon and Colette left to return to London and Ella set to on the washing up. The greasy water had gone cold and she drained it away before refilling the bowl. She was thankful all her crockery was still in tact. It was six o'clock and Ella was so tired but she didn't want to go back to bed and the house was too quiet to sleep. She switched on the TV in the kitchen and put on a news channel so she would have the company of their normal everyday business voices and then curled up on her favourite armchair by the window.

A tap on the window of the back door jolted Ella awake and she turned stiffly in her armchair to see Libby peering in with a concerned look on her face and a bowl of something in her hands. Slowly and painfully she unfolded her rigid limbs, glancing at the clock to see she'd been asleep for a couple of hours. She hobbled across the kitchen and unlocked the door.

"Hello Ella. Are you alright? You don't look at all well. Shall I call the doctor?" Libby put a bowl of strawberries on the table.

"No, I'm fine, really. I've just had a bad night that's all." Ella felt even more tired than before she'd fallen asleep. "Can you stop for a cup of tea?"

"I tell you what, you sit back down and I'll do it, you really don't look very well. Are you sure you're ok?"

Ella explained in more detail than she intended, what had happened in the last twenty-four hours. Libby listened, genuinely concerned.

"It makes you think, doesn't it? How lucky we really are to have our families and our health without even thinking about the lovely homes we have and the beautiful place we live in. We take much too much for granted." Libby stared out the window, lost for a second in her own worries but aware this wasn't the time to confide in Ella. She brought herself back to the present moment, leaned across the table and squeezed Ella's hand. Several stock phrases of the correct thing to say were forming in her mind, how everything would be alright or that things would work themselves out but Libby stopped herself. Sometimes there just weren't any words that could help and it was more genuine to simply say nothing at all.

Libby took the bowl of strawberries in her hands. "Anyway, the reason I came over was to bring you these, freshly picked from my garden this morning. You need to make sure you're getting your vitamins." She pushed the bowl towards Ella.

Ella picked up on the last comment about vitamins, not sure whether Libby was being specific or just generally reminding her to look after herself.

"Thanks, they look delicious. You're always so busy, all I've done since Colette left is wander around, sleep and worry."

"Well, that isn't going to help anyone, really, is it?"

"No, I know, but I can't help it. I wish I could go back and be with her. But I suppose that's not really appropriate, is it?"

"Not really. And anyway, you can't just go gallivanting around the country – you need to look after yourself at the moment." Libby raised her eyebrows, knowingly. Ella didn't protest or question the remark, they simply held each other's gaze and that was proof enough to Libby she was right in her assumptions. The silence hung in the air like a secret language between them.

Libby smiled, pleased with herself. "Well, I hope Dr Cookson is looking after you well," she said smiling, unable to keep the glint from her eyes.

"Erm, yes, he is."

"Good. And I should think so too." Libby laughed.

Oh crikey, she thinks Neil is the father, Ella realised. She tried to think of something to say but just couldn't think quick enough.

"Right I'm off. I just wanted to give you the fruit while it's fresh. I'm off to see Andrew, he's invited me to lunch. It's been ages since we had lunch together. I'm really looking forward to it. See you later, you take care."

Libby let herself out and once again Ella was alone with her thoughts. She hadn't seen Andrew for a few days and couldn't help wondering why he and Libby were all of a sudden going for lunch together. Her concern was that Libby would mention her suspicions about Ella being pregnant to Andrew. It didn't bear thinking about. And if she did, what would his reaction be? And what would Libby's reaction be, to Andrew's reaction? Ella felt sick, for completely different reasons to the normal sickness she had felt some weeks earlier. She felt a sharp pain in her side and suddenly felt weak as if her legs were going to give way underneath her. Libby's words came back to her, as if in warning, "You need to look after yourself, at the moment." She certainly did. The following few weeks could be traumatic enough in helping Colette to deal with whatever was coming her way, and she needed to rest and conserve her energy if she was to be of help to anyone. There was also the worry of who was going to be around for her when she needed help in the coming months.

Chapter Twenty-Three

Libby woke on the morning of the mid-summer party to crystal clear blue skies, not a hint of a cloud in sight. She was smiling before she even got up. She went down to the kitchen and made herself a cup of coffee, taking it back upstairs to enjoy in bed. Libby knew this was probably the only quiet time she would get to herself today. She passed her children's bedrooms, their doors closed, glad for once they were still lying-in. There was so much to do today and once it all got going, she knew there would be no let up until late into the night. Even so, she felt calm and relaxed, confident in the knowledge that everything was organised and ready for the day. It was going to be just perfect.

Libby pulled the curtains and knew instinctively it was going to be a gloriously hot day. She could tell from over twenty years of waking to this view every morning. She knew by the gentle movement of the waves and the way the sunlight played on the surface of the water creating thousands of sparkling crystals. Her outfit looked gorgeous, ironed and hanging up ready for her to slip into it later in the day. It was incredibly expensive and she knew she shouldn't have bought it but it was difficult to resist when she had never had to before.

After a quick shower, Libby scribbled a note for Todd and Jess, reminding them of the list of things she wanted them to do this morning; empty the dish-washer and make sure the glasses were polished before putting them away, vacuum the downstairs and clear away any stray CDs, school books, shoes, clothes and anything else that belonged in their bedrooms. She then drove over to Francine's to see to last minute details and make sure everything was coming together as it should be.

Francine was not there when Libby arrived but there were several other people wandering around and Libby got stuck in straightaway; dealing with the delivery of flowers and directing vans and people to their respective directions. Finally Francine appeared swishing to a halt on the gravel drive, abandoning her car in what was quite an inconvenient place, thought Libby, although she didn't like to say anything.

"Morning Libby. God, that feels better. I've just been for an aromatherapy massage and facial. I feel human again."

Libby slightly begrudgingly wished she had time today for a massage and facial but at least Francine was making an effort for the day. Anyway, her indulgent pampering seemed to have put her in a good mood.

"You must be ready for a refreshment break. Come on in and we'll find something fizzy."

Libby followed Francine through to her huge kitchen which made Libby's own look like a doll's house by comparison. Francine took a bottle of champagne from what looked like a walk-in fridge; she took two glasses in one hand and went back outside to the garden terrace. They were met by Roger coming from the opposite direction, obviously with the same thing in mind.

"Excellent idea, just what I need."

"And you're just in time to do the honours." Francine handed him the bottle to open. Roger swiftly removed the foil and wire before deftly but gently popping the cork. Libby was impressed and wondered how many times he'd done that before. He handed Libby a glass.

"I've just been sorting out your seating people," he said.

"Oh, was there a problem?"

"There was very nearly a bun fight between them and your florist. Bit of a clash over space." He noticed Libby's concerned expression. "It's ok," he laughed. "It's all sorted now. Didn't even come to fisticuffs. Sit back, relax, and enjoy your drink."

Libby did sit back. She enjoyed her drink and the rather splendid view of Roger and his relaxed manner which seemed to have an intoxicating yet calming effect on her. Once again, his presence added an extra dimension of excitement to the evening's festivities. He was so attentive to her, his softly spoken voice, caring and considerate. Libby looked across at Francine who seemed miles away, staring out beyond the garden but at nothing in particular. Not for the first time, Libby noted her apparent indifference to her gorgeous husband. He offered her another glass of champagne and while she knew she shouldn't, midday drinking always went straight to her head, she was enjoying herself too much to refuse. She convinced herself that a quick afternoon nap would refresh her.

Libby arrived home to find Todd and Jess had gone out and much to her annoyance they hadn't even started on their chores.

Libby assumed that after the festivities at Francine's had finished, a few friends would come back with her to continue the partying, probably into the early hours – and she wanted the house clean and tidy. She could really have done with Mrs O'Brien's help but she had gone away for her usual two-week break in August to The Lake District to visit her sister. Todd and Jess had better have a good reason for letting her down. There was still lots to do and now she wouldn't have time to take a much needed nap. She felt tired and grumpy already. Libby set to straight away, emptying the dishwasher then vacuuming throughout. She opened the back door to let in some fresh air and noticed the sun had disappeared behind what looked horribly like storm clouds although it was still hot making it far too humid and uncomfortable to do housework. "That's all we need", she muttered, "for it to rain. It'll be a great party with a muddy floor in a damp marquee."

Ella took her time getting ready. She didn't feel too good, she felt tired and sluggish and not at all in the mood for a party. Andrew was picking her up early at six-thirty, collecting Libby from next door first. He had phoned yesterday to make arrangements and she had thanked her lucky stars he hadn't said anything about the baby. It was good to know she could trust Libby with her secret although she knew she would have to tell Andrew, and soon.

Ella wore her powder blue jeans that she'd never worn before as they had always been a little too big. They fitted snugly now and she added a pretty white vest with a blue angora cardigan, decorated with crystal beads around the hem and cuffs. She was ready in good time and waited in the garden where it was slightly cooler, looking dubiously at the darkening sky.

Libby dashed from room to room, grabbing armfuls of her children's bits and pieces that didn't belong. She didn't have time to keep running up and down to their bedrooms so she tossed the whole lot into the cupboard under the stairs.

She was running disastrously late and didn't have anywhere near the time she'd intended to get herself ready. The long luxurious bath she'd planned was replaced with a five-minute shower. She tried to dry herself but it was so humid in the house she still felt hot and clammy. She didn't want to put her dress on yet and so applied her make-up in just her underwear constantly checking her watch and cursing her children for being wherever they were instead of home as agreed. They were to come along to the party later and Libby needed to go over the travel arrangements with them.

The sound of the kitchen door opening meant they were home at last. Libby could hear their voices. She couldn't hear what they were saying but it sounded like a serious debate, their voices urgent and commanding and then someone switched on the vacuum cleaner. Libby tutted, irritated, and grabbed her bath robe from the bathroom door pulling it round her as she rushed downstairs.

In the kitchen she came face to face with a confused looking Jess who was peering into the empty dishwasher. She looked at her mum as if she'd lost the plot.

"It's already empty!"

"Yes, that's because I emptied it earlier! And I've also done the vacuuming. Todd, stop that." Libby shouted above the noise and dashed into the lounge but Todd was engrossed with his back to her and didn't hear. Libby shouted some more and then, exasperated, finally pulled the plug from its socket. A bewildered Todd turned to see what had happened.

"Todd, I've already done that."

"Then why did you put it on the list?" said Todd, getting annoyed himself.

Libby didn't give the obvious answer to her son but merely glared at him for being insolent. It had the desired effect and Todd began re-winding the cable. Libby sighed heavily and returned to the kitchen. Jess had obviously picked up on her mother's mood and had done the sensible thing by disappearing out of sight. Libby looked at her watch, she had just minutes to finish getting ready before Andrew arrived. Unfortunately, he was never late. She fancied a cup of tea but didn't even have time for that. She opened the fridge and noticed an open bottle of wine, poured herself a small half glass and then realising there was just a small amount left, not worth leaving in the bottle, she filled the glass completely.

Back upstairs, she knocked on Jess's door and walked in to see her daughter belly down on her bed deep in conversation on her mobile phone and not even noticing her mother in the room. She opened Todd's door to see he was in exactly the same position.

Totally oblivious and unhelpful, both of them, Libby muttered as she left his room.

In her own bedroom Libby sat on the edge of her bed, closed her eyes and tried to calm herself for a few seconds. She took a few sips of wine and tried to relax, reassuring herself that even if she wasn't ready when Andrew arrived, it wouldn't be the end of the world if he had to wait for a few minutes. But she really didn't want to be late for Francine. Libby had said she would be there by seven o'clock. As she thought of Francine and the party and guests arriving, her thoughts quickly led to the fact that Roger would be there too. She liked Roger. If all else failed tonight, he would be good company. She felt instantly better, her flustered five minutes over.

Libby finished dressing, gave her make-up one final check and was just putting her lipstick and perfume into her evening bag as she heard the familiar sound of Andrew's car on the drive. She quickly drained her glass of wine and just as she got to the kitchen, Andrew appeared at the back door. She held up a finger indicating she would be one minute and Andrew sign-languaged back, mouthing and pointing, which she took to mean he would go and see if Ella was ready. Libby tore a page from a notebook and scribbled a note to Jess and Todd, repeating the arrangements about who would be picking them up and at what time. She taped the note to the biscuit tin which she placed strategically in the middle of the worktop, knowing one or the other of her children would be digging into it pretty swiftly as soon as she had left the house.

Andrew met Ella halfway to her cottage as she was already on her way down the lane to Libby's.

"I thought I heard your car," she said. Andrew swiftly enfolded her in his arms and kissed her warmly but discreetly, smiling as he released her. She was glad of his embrace and had missed his physical presence over the last couple of weeks.

"I think Libby is almost ready. And you look lovely by the way." Andrew turned to look fully at Ella by his side, and was concerned to see her clutching her abdomen, her face grimacing as if in pain.

"Ella? What's wrong?"

"Mm, nothing." Ella closed her eyes and tried her hardest to remain calm and conceal everything even though she was tempted to blurt it out right there and then, including all her worst and unthinkable fears about what this pain might be. And then as quick as it had come, it was gone.

"Ah, that's better. Probably just indigestion."

Andrew laughed. "Have you been eating too many pies?"

Ella laughed along, but a little nervously, wondering if Andrew was alluding to her putting on weight, but still she said nothing. They arrived at Libby's house just as Libby was coming down the path to meet them.

"Libby, you look lovely. What a gorgeous dress," said Ella, admiring her friend's exquisite outfit. She had obviously made a real effort for tonight and Ella felt a little shabby now in her jeans and cardigan.

"Yes, you do," agreed Andrew, raising his eyebrows in exaggerated admiration.

"Thank-you, thank-you," said Libby, feeling herself redden at all the compliments and maybe also due to the amount of wine she had consumed during the day. She linked arms with Andrew, boosted by his attention, happy with the world, her outfit and life in general. She was ready for the magic of the evening to begin.

Andrew parked the car on an adjoining field, as directed by a young warden. They walked towards the house, through the magnificent gardens to where the marquee was sited on the lawn. Guests were milling about outside and avoiding entering the marquee which was hot and humid inside.

Roger and Francine were standing at the entrance to the marquee and spotted Libby and her friends as they approached.

"Ah, here she is, the lady of the day." Roger placed his hands gently on Libby's shoulders and kissed her cheek. "You've done a fantastic job. We're very grateful – aren't we Francine?" Roger turned back to his wife who agreed, not quite as enthusiastically as her husband and maybe even a little begrudgingly, thought Libby.

"Yes, Libby, it's all very nice."

Libby knew she was blushing from the kiss from Roger and hoped no-one had noticed. And anyway it was a very warm evening.

Libby introduced Ella to Roger and Francine as they walked into the marquee. Ella was amazed, she felt as if she had walked into a magic fairyland. Extravagant swathes of pink and silver fabric were draped all around the marquee. There were gorgeous displays of fresh flowers in bright summer colours of pink and white and lime green and the tables were stylishly decorated with sparkly silver covers, silver candles and a simple centrepiece of white roses. It was beautiful. Libby had done an amazing job. Ella looked across at Libby to tell her so but she was chatting away with Roger and she couldn't catch her attention.

Roger was opening a bottle of champagne. The cork burst upwards, thudding on the marquee fabric as they cheered his efforts.

"Here we go." Roger poured Libby's glass first, which didn't go unnoticed by Francine who stood with her empty glass in hand, silently daring him not to pour her drink next. Fortunately for him, he made the right decision and poured Francine a glass.

"Ella, grab a glass."

"No, no, none for me, please. I'll just have some water."

"Ah come on, this is a party. Special occasion. You've got to have some champers. Or what about a Bucks Fizz instead? How about that?"

"No really, I'd rather not. I'll just have the orange juice."

Roger observed Ella's firm tone and realised she was not to be persuaded. He eased off. It wasn't appropriate to pressure someone into having a drink.

Libby watched the interaction, admiring Roger for his sensitivity, and giving Ella a knowing look.

Ella sipped her juice. It was incredibly hot in the marquee and the niggling pain in her belly was still bothering her. She constantly analysed it, was it getting stronger or easing up a little? Could it be just something and nothing or was it serious? At odd moments, she wasn't even sure if it was there at all, maybe it was just her imagination. They moved over to a table with a good view of the stage and the dance floor. Ella was relieved to be able to sit down and felt a little more comfortable. The band began playing and the music acted as an announcement that the party had really begun and the marquee was soon filling up with people. A large queue had gathered at the bar but Roger made sure their table was constantly attended to by the waiting staff. He no longer encouraged

Ella with the champagne but kept topping up her glass with fresh orange juice.

Ella noticed that Libby kept looking at her watch before looking anxiously at the entrance to the marquee. Suddenly her face relaxed into a smile as she got up from her seat and waved to attract the attention of Todd and Jess who had just arrived. She pulled over a couple of stray chairs and fussed over her children, getting them drinks and checking that they had no problems on the journey.

The dance floor was soon filling up, mainly with toddlers in pretty party dresses and girls not much older in their best trendy gear. Ella smiled at the scene, glad she had such a good view. The music was loud, too loud to be able to talk and for this Ella was grateful. Andrew was sitting to one side of her and a couple who she didn't know were on the other. She didn't feel like engaging in small talk and was glad for the excuse just to be able to listen to the music and watch the dancing which was getting crazier by the second. The combination of heat and alcohol was causing people to lose their inhibitions fast.

Ella noticed Andrew laughing and looked over to the cause of his amusement. Roger had Libby by both hands and was pulling her out of her seat onto the dance floor. Libby half-heartedly resisted for a second but then gave in and followed him into the lively crowd, obviously delighted. Ella laughed too but instinctively looked across the table to gauge Francine's reaction. She wasn't there which Ella thought was probably a good thing.

The band was playing a selection of country songs, creating a fantastic party atmosphere. The dancers on the floor were linking arms and swinging round with great enthusiasm and a lot of foot stomping and ye-haaing. Roger was swinging poor Libby almost off her feet, as she squealed and giggled, not sure whether she was more scared or thrilled. Ella was tempted to get up and join in but she reckoned she was safer sitting down so she had to content herself with some serious toe-tapping and clapping along with the rest of the audience who couldn't or weren't brave enough to get up. Roger and Libby continued their dancing for another couple of songs and then finally returned to the table, Libby quite out of puff and very red in the face. Roger poured her another glass of champagne. She'd lost count of how many she'd had a while ago.

It was getting dark outside and Ella noticed as the natural light gradually faded, hundreds of tiny white fairy lights were appearing across the ceiling of the marquee. They were incredibly pretty and magical, thought Ella, as she continued to gaze up, mesmerised by the tiny shiny stars, dancing and shimmering in the distance. It was the sound of Andrew's voice that brought her back down to earth.

"Not drinking and not dancing either? Are you not well?" He was smiling as he spoke, which reassured Ella his question wasn't serious.

"I'm just feeling lazy actually. Anyway, I'm enjoying the show." The music was still very loud and they were shouting to be heard.

"Do you fancy a walk?" said Andrew.

"Mm. Good idea." The idea of some cool, fresh air was very appealing.

They strolled through the garden towards the house. A long drawn out rumble just about audible in the distance broke the silence.

"Was that thunder?" Ella looked at the sky as if expecting confirmation.

"Yes, I think it was." Andrew joined her in her sky-stare. It was completely black, not a star to be seen, the sky was dark with thick heavy storm clouds.

Ella wanted to tell Andrew what she knew she must tell him soon but she just couldn't find the right words to start the conversation. She was relieved when he said he needed to go to the bathroom. This would give her a couple of extra minutes alone to think seriously about what she should say. They went into the house through a side door propped open which led into a small hallway. Jess came out of the bathroom, her face was a tell-tale shade of greeny-white and the way she tried to avoid eye-contact with her grandfather suggested perhaps she had had too much champagne. She slunk back outside to the garden without saying a word. Ella and Andrew exchanged glances together with a little humble smile that said 'been there, done that.'

Ella waited in the adjoining conservatory. The blinds were pulled down, protecting the room from the heat earlier in the day. There was just one window in the middle which didn't have its blind drawn, the window was open to let in some air. Ella peered through to the floodlit garden, a few people had escaped the sweltering heat of the marquee and were milling around enjoying the still evening and cocking their heads as the low rumbles of thunder continued. Suddenly, she spotted Libby right outside the window, heading towards the main entrance to the house. Ella tapped on the glass, Libby looked up and smiled, changing her direction to go to meet her. Ella wanted to congratulate her on organising such a fantastic evening but she wasn't sure Libby was in a state to listen.

"Libby, are you ok?"

"I'm fine, honestly. Just a little bit too much champagne but don't worry, I'm not about to fall over backwards in the flowerbeds. Wouldn't want to –." Libby tried to say 'humiliate' but after three attempts at the word, she flapped her hands and gave up. "Don't want to make a fool of myself, is what I'm trying to say."

"Well I'm sure you won't. As long as you're ok, that's good then."

"I'm ok but are you ok?" Libby's voice was a little louder than Ella was comfortable with and she was nervous of what Libby would say next.

"You're a good girl for not drinking. It's the right thing to do. But I think a bit of dancing would be alright." Libby wobbled over closer to Ella. "That wee little baby won't object to his mother having a bit of a song and dance – he'll probably love it. Ooh, do you think it's a boy or a girl? It's all so exciting." Libby put her arms around Ella and gave her a hug. Ella was lost for words. Libby had been blocking her view to the doorway but now she moved in for her hug, Ella could see over the top of her head and her heart sank. Andrew was standing there, wide-eyed in surprise. Ella deduced he'd been standing there for a while.

Libby finally pulled back, as Andrew entered the room.

"Hello Andrew. Are you having fun?"

"Hello Libby. Yes, it's a good evening." Andrew suddenly looked very serious. Libby didn't notice.

"Now, I was on my way to find that lovely Roger man. We were having such a good time and then he disappeared on me." Libby tottered out of the room, banging her shin on a low table and grabbing the back of an armchair to steady herself.

Andrew moved slowly towards Ella, each holding the other's gaze, not sure who should or would speak first.

Andrew held her hands firmly in his. "Well. This explains one or two things."

"Andrew, I've wanted to tell you. I was planning to tell you now, right now, while we were walking."

"It's ok."

"And Libby just guessed, she put two and two together."

"Yes, she's good at that."

"But nobody else knows – I haven't told anyone – apart from Colette, of course."

"Does Libby know it's me?"

"No – she thinks it's Neil Cookson's."

"Mm." Andrew gently kissed the top of her forehead.

"This is what you want isn't it?"

"Yes it is, but I didn't plan it. I wasn't even thinking about it." Ella was desperate to explain she hadn't tried to trap him. But there was no need.

"I know, I know. It's ok. You'll be a fantastic mother."

"Are you ok with this?"

"A bit shocked but we can talk later." Andrew held her in his arms, Ella reached up to hold him close, resting her head against his broad chest, she turned her head to the side leaning her cheek against him for a few seconds. She was facing the window, the one that didn't have the blind drawn. There was someone out there, looking in. Whoever it was, was a little way off but coming towards the conservatory now.

"Oh my god" whispered Ella, "it's Libby."

Andrew and Ella were standing apart by the time Libby had come back inside. Her face was red, her anger clear to see, but her voice was surprisingly quiet.

"You bitch. What have you been up to?"

"Libby, we need to talk but not like this. I think we should – .""

"I don't care what you think! Coming here, messing with people's lives."

Ella could feel herself getting riled. The pain in her side was getting worse and her head was pounding with unwanted thoughts, full of fear. She didn't need this. But Libby wasn't giving up yet.

"You dirty tart."

"Libby, that's enough," said Andrew gently. A little too gently thought Ella, who really had had enough, tiredness and anxiety preventing her from keeping control.

"You think you're so perfect? Hardly!" said Ella.

"What are you going on about?"

"You want to take a look at yourself. You're not so perfect. Take a look at your precious children, for one thing." She regretted her words the second she'd spoken them. And to make things even worse, she noticed Jess hovering in the doorway, obviously not straying too far away from the bathroom. She stepped tentatively into the room, looking like a frightened sparrow, looking between her mum and Ella.

Ella couldn't bear any more of this. She just wanted to get home. Libby attempted to storm off but the effect was tampered to some extent due to the fact that she needed the support of her daughter as she stumbled out of the room.

"Ella, are you ok? You mustn't pay any attention, she's had too much to drink."

"I know that. I'm going home now."

"Do you want me to give you a lift?"

"Are you allowed?" snapped Ella.

"If you would like me to give you a lift home, then I will," Andrew said simply.

"Yes please. I'd be grateful if you would.

"Wait here, I'll bring the car round, I'll meet you on the drive in a couple of minutes."

The pain in Ella's side was definitely getting stronger, this was not in her mind, although she did wonder if the stress from what had just happened was making her feel worse. She just wanted to get back to the familiarity of her cottage and relax in her own homely surroundings and hopefully this pain and discomfort would go away.

Ella stood in front of the open window trying to breathe herself calm. She could hear the voice of someone speaking into a microphone, coming from the marquee. They were probably calling the raffle and announcing the donations to the charity. She was glad she'd finally decided what to do with Todd's ill gotten gains and very happy to have the money out of the house. Donating it to the charity anonymously was the obvious thing to do. She would tell Todd about it in a few days and hopefully it would be an end to it and he would leave her alone. The voice had stopped and now there was clapping and cheering and then the band started up again. Ella had a clear view of the marquee across the other side of the garden and she saw two figures emerge at the entrance. One of them ran as fast as he could across the lawn, onto the gravel footpath and towards the house. The second person, a young girl, was struggling to keep up. Ella suddenly recognised Todd and Jess and stepped back from the window out of sight although it made no difference, they knew she was there. A distinct growl of thunder meant the storm was creeping closer. She heard someone clatter into the hallway and then Todd appeared in the doorway, leaning against the frame, breathing hard. A few seconds later, Jess appeared but she was hanging back. She looked scared which in turn made Ella feel uneasy. Todd's tall, gangly body was blocking the exit.

"That was my money, wasn't it?" His voice was low and menacing.

Ella turned her back on him. She needed to get out of this room, Andrew would be waiting for her, but she knew the best thing was to keep calm.

"Not now Todd." She took a few steps into the room but Todd was behind her in a split second. He meant to grab her arm, to make her turn round to face him and admit she'd given his money away but Ella pre-empted his move and jerked herself away from him. It all happened so quickly. She tripped over the rug and fell heavily and awkwardly onto a small table before landing on the floor.

Todd was standing over her, still angry but not sure now what to do. Jess came forward, just inside the room. Her shaky voice barely above a whisper although Ella heard her words distinctly and the urgency in them.

"Todd, careful! She's pregnant."

Todd just stared confused at the thought of his grandad and Ella being parents together. Ella had pulled herself up and was sitting on a wicker armchair, breathless and shocked.

"Is she ok?" whispered Jess, still hovering by the doorway.

"Are you ok?" asked Todd, gently now, all the fight gone from him.

Ella couldn't look at him, she simply nodded hoping he would just go away. Todd looked across at his younger sister for confirmation of what they should do next. Telepathically they decided they should leave. Ella gave it a few seconds before looking through the window. She saw Todd and Jess sloping off towards the marquee, heads down, not talking. Ella left the house and made her way down the garden to the drive to meet Andrew. She was ok apart from feeling a little shaky. She was trying to reassure herself there was no damage done although the nagging pain in her side was still there.

Libby was lost; she'd gone into the house in search of Roger not realising how much of a rabbit warren it was. She was sure she'd come through this hallway at least three times now. Irritated that she would have to abandon her search, Libby turned to go back outside to the marquee. The sound of chinking glass from a room off somewhere to her right, made her pause. She investigated along a narrow side corridor and could hear music playing softly. She followed the sound, and entered a room at the end of the corridor where she was delighted to find Roger, helping himself to whiskey from a decanter.

"Hello, I've been looking for you," she said suggestively.

The small room was obviously his private office with a large desk to one side and rows of shelves filled with legal books.

"This is cosy," she said, perching herself on the edge of the desk.

"Drink?" offered Roger, who was also quite the worse for wear.

"Yes, champagne please."

"Whiskey or whiskey, I'm afraid."

"Well, a whiskey would be lovely. As are you Roger."

Roger handed her a glass and filled it with a measure. They chinked glasses and each took a swig.

"Uurgh! I don't like whiskey," said Libby giggling and banging her glass down onto the desk. "I do like you though!" Libby reached up and put her arms around Roger's neck, tilting her face up towards his, closing her eyes in anticipation of a passionate, lingering kiss.

"Ah, Libby, no." He tried to release her hands from behind his neck and as he did so, the whiskey glass slipped from his fingers and smashed into the fireplace onto the stone hearth. Libby tightened her fingers in a vice-like grip about his neck and to make it all worse, Roger was sure he could hear his wife's voice calling his name.

"Roger?" She pushed open the door. "What the hell?"

Libby felt his forceful strength as Roger prised her hands apart and away from him. She was confused; she thought this was what he was after. He'd been coming on to her all evening, hadn't he?

"Get your hands off my husband."

"Calm down Fran. No harm done. The old girl's had too much champagne. She just needs some strong coffee, that's all."

Libby was horrified. She wasn't that inebriated. She pushed herself away from the desk, bolting for the door, but her legs wouldn't work properly and she only got halfway across the room before falling into an armchair, sitting bent over with her head in her hands.

Francine noticed the smashed glass in the hearth, noting it was from an expensive set - a gift from someone or other. She gave her husband a cold, disapproving look and on her way out of the room said, "I'll send through some coffee. And then perhaps you ought to ring for a taxi."

For a split second Roger thought he was being turfed out of his own home, and the puzzled look on his face obviously conveyed the thought.

"For her!" snapped Francine as she left the room, muttering to herself.

Andrew pulled up outside Ella's cottage and parked on the drive. "I'll see you in Ella, do you fancy a chat over a cup of coffee?"

"Not tonight Andrew, do you mind? I don't feel too good and I'm really tired. I'm going straight up."

"No of course I don't mind. Is there anything I can do?"

"No, thanks anyway, I just need a good nights sleep. I'll be fine tomorrow." It was clear to them both that the essence of their relationship was changing fast.

Ella undressed slowly hoping to minimise the pain. She'd made some chamomile tea and eased herself gently into bed, leaning back against the propped up pillows, sinking into their comfort and breathing a sigh of relief as she found herself able to relax. She looked at her book on the bedside cupboard but knew she wouldn't be able to concentrate. She decided to just lie back and relax for a while, drink her tea and hopefully everything would be better tomorrow.

Andrew was tempted to drive straight home but thought he ought to return to the party to check on Libby. Flickers of lightening lit the sky followed a few seconds later by the thunder as the rain slowly began. Large, heavy blobs of water hit the windscreen like splattering insects.

Andrew parked on the drive outside Francine's house. It was getting late and many people had left already. He noticed Libby sitting on a garden bench, near the entrance to the drive and walked back down. She had Todd and Jess on either side of her and they were all ridiculously wet. The rain was hammering down and there was nowhere close by for them to shelter. Todd had his arm protectively around his mother. As Andrew got closer, he could see and hear Libby was upset about something.

"Libby? What's going on? What are you all doing out here?"

"Mum doesn't feel well, that's all," said Jess quietly.

"We're waiting for a taxi," said Todd. Andrew didn't need to ask why Libby didn't feel well. That was evident some time ago. And there was no point in making a fuss now. The children were quiet and bewildered and he didn't want to add to their discomfort. Libby continued to sniff noisily into a crumbling tissue, avoiding eye contact with Andrew.

"Looks like this is your taxi now. Do you want me to come with you?"

Libby got up from the bench, still a little unsteady on her feet and got into the taxi without saying a word. Only Todd looked back at Andrew, giving him a sad half smile. Andrew watched them drive off and then turned back to the direction of the marquee. He could hear music and the laughter from the last of the revellers determined to keep going until the end but suddenly Andrew realised he didn't want to be anywhere near their joviality and drunken silliness. He turned and went straight back to his car. He was looking forward to the quiet sanctuary of his home, and enjoying one or two brandies in peaceful and contented solitude.

The sound of a car door woke Ella and instinctively she turned to look at the clock. She'd fallen asleep propped up against her pillows for about half an hour. At first she thought it was the car's headlights lighting up her bedroom but the simultaneous blast of thunder indicated the storm was directly overhead. Through the noise of the rain on the window, she could just about hear the car slowly turning before driving off. It must be Libby returning from the party, Ella realised. She looked at the clock again. It was only eleven-thirty; she would've expected her to be much later than this, imagined she would be one of the very last to leave having stayed to thank everyone and say good-bye to each and everyone personally. Ella strained to hear but she couldn't hear any voices from the posse of friends she imagined would have come back to Libby's home after the party.

She thought she could hear Todd's deep teenage monotone but she couldn't be sure. It wasn't a good sign if Libby had come home early and alone, and Ella's heart sank as she recalled other memories of the evening. She pulled her pillows down flat and settled down hoping she could quickly get back to sleep.

Chapter Twenty-Four

Libby heard the siren in the distance, not paying much attention to it until it got louder, meaning much closer, until it was so loud, it was as if it were outside her own front door. She looked along the lane and saw the ambulance park high up on Ella's drive. They weren't inside for long. Libby watched discreetly from an upstairs window as Ella was stretchered into the ambulance, seconds later it sped off again, with lights flashing and siren screeching.

That was early this morning and Libby was beside herself with anguish. So far, she'd managed to busy herself with endless household chores. All manner of mindless jobs were getting done just to keep her mind occupied. She would have liked to be out in the garden but the rain continued to fall unrelenting from a solid grey sky. Libby stared through the kitchen window at nothing in particular and then jumped as Andrew appeared at the door and let himself in.

"Oh Andrew, thank god you're here. I wasn't sure if you were still speaking to me after yesterday."

"Don't be daft Libby. How are you feeling?"

"Oh I'm fine, really." Libby's head was thumping but she didn't feel she was in any position to complain. "I've phoned you, a couple of times, but there was no answer."

"It seems to be the fashion. I've been phoning Ella but she's not answering."

"How is she? Please say everything's ok. What do you mean, you've been phoning her?"

"What do you mean, how is she?"

"Oh god Andrew. Ella's been taken to hospital. I just assumed you were with her. I thought neither of you were talking to me and I wouldn't blame you."

"When was all this?"

"This morning."

"Have you got the phone number for the hospital?"

"Yes, it's here. I tried ringing but I was stupid and I didn't think quick enough and said I was her neighbour. The said they couldn't really tell me anything as I wasn't family. They just said she was ok but wouldn't say anything more. And that doesn't mean anything does it? I mean, what about the baby?"

Andrew calmly held up his hands and then placed them firmly on Libby's shoulders, putting his forehead to hers. "Sshh now. I'll phone the hospital and we'll find out what's what."

Libby left Andrew in the kitchen to make his phone call, going into the lounge to give him some privacy but still keeping an ear out for what he would say. She could hear the deep rumblings of his voice but not his exact words. She moved nearer to the hallway door, just in time to hear Andrew say, "Yes, I am, sort of. Actually I'm the baby's father. Yes, I realise that but I've only just found out. Is she allowed visitors?"

Andrew fidgeted on the spot and turned to see Libby's head poking out of the lounge doorway. Their eyes met and Libby smiled feebly at being caught out and Andrew smiled back, jerking his head indicating she should come back into the kitchen. Libby put the kettle on as Andrew finished his call.

"Ok, thank-you anyway." Andrew put down the phone and turned to Libby. He looked weary, she thought.

"The person I spoke to can't tell me anything. They suggest I phone again later."

Andrew perched on the edge of a stool and rubbed his eyes. There were a hundred and one questions Libby was desperate to ask but after everything that had happened over the last few days and seeing how tired Andrew looked, she managed to resist the urge and keep quiet. She made the tea in silence, placed the mugs on the worktop and sat down next to him. Andrew sighed, long and deep. "I really don't know where I go from here." Again Libby withheld the many comments she wanted to make but waited patiently instead, hoping Andrew would continue.

"Perhaps you should go to the hospital. They'll have to tell you what's going on then."

"I'm not sure. Ella obviously hasn't asked for me. I don't really know what to do. Do you mind if I wait here for a while?"

"No, of course not." Libby was relieved that all seemed to be back to normal between her and Andrew. She wasn't at all sure anything would ever be normal between her and Ella.

They drank more tea but the conversation was slow. Andrew was thoughtful and while Libby was resolved to let him alone for a while, it was becoming hard work. As a distraction and to occupy herself, she prepared an elaborate lunch of asparagus tortilla and green salad with a blue cheese dressing. She put a plate of delicious looking food in front of Andrew and he muttered something Libby could just about hear. It sounded like he said just a simple sandwich would have done. Andrew picked at his meal and Libby had lost her appetite too. She made yet another cup of tea but neither of them drank it.

After an interminable time, they heard a car pull up nearby. They looked at each other, both surprised and without speaking, agreed this would be Ella arriving home. In a taxi presumably, thought Andrew, a little dejected. Mysteriously, two car doors slammed. Andrew went through to the conservatory at the side of the house, closely followed by Libby and they peered along the lane towards Ella's cottage. They recognised the little sports car immediately.

"He is her doctor," said Libby softly.

"Doctors offer taxi services these days do they? I thought it was difficult enough to get an appointment."

Libby didn't really know what to say. She wondered if Andrew's sarcasm was aimed at her. He knew she had tried getting Ella and Neil together as a couple but now it all seemed so horribly complicated.

"Right, I'm off." Libby knew what he meant. He was off home and he wasn't going to go next door to see Ella.

"Andrew –"

"Libby, leave it. Just leave things." He shut the door roughly behind him, not quite a slam, but not far off.

Libby violently loaded the dishwasher and slammed the door shut. She heard the sound of Neil Cookson's car driving off. Ella would be on her own now and Libby desperately wanted to know if she and the baby were ok. She went through to the conservatory and looked up the lane towards Ella's cottage. She wanted to pop in like she always did but she wasn't brave enough, not after all the terrible things she had said.

Ella watched as Neil Cookson ran to his car in the rain then closed the door. She hoped he didn't think her rude for not offering him a cup of tea – somehow she didn't think he would. It was kind of him to give her a lift home. She'd been waiting for a taxi outside the hospital when by chance he'd come out just after her. He could tell just by looking at her that this wasn't a routine check-up. Ella's explanation, in one sentence, confirmed his suspicions. She wasn't looking forward to the drive home with a chatty taxi driver and gratefully accepted Neil's offer of a lift. He understood her need for quiet and they travelled in easy, not uncomfortable, silence.

Ella lay down on the settee, not even wanting the sound of the television for company. She had to think for a few seconds to determine what day it was. Only Sunday. Yesterday and the party and everything, all seemed like ages ago. Tomorrow would be Danielle's funeral. So much death and grieving. Poor Jon. And poor Colette. Ella lay her head down on a cushion totally overwhelmed by the prospect of how long her own grieving would last. How long would it take to get over the loss of the baby she never thought she would have – probably forever. Her last thought before falling asleep was of Andrew, she knew she should tell him. She would do it later.

Libby finally served the roast at seven o'clock. It was a bit late for Sunday lunch but she hadn't been able to organise herself all morning. Even the children were subdued on hearing the news that Ella had been taken to hospital. She started cooking late afternoon more as a way of occupying herself than anything else, and then Andrew had phoned a short while ago to say Ella had miscarried the baby.

Libby, Todd and Jess took their places around the dining room table in silence, staring at the impressive meal in front of them. A roast gammon joint cooked to perfection, crispy roast potatoes as well as new potatoes with a butter and mustard dressing and a choice of fresh vegetables. There was far too much of everything, laid out in serving dishes. Libby watched as Jess slowly helped herself to one slice of meat, one potato and a few carrots and then Todd, who could usually eat for the country, served himself a similar plate.

"Come on you two, eat up. I spent ages on this." Libby served herself generous helpings of everything but after just a few mouthfuls she had to concede that she had no appetite either.

"Is it ok if we leave now?" asked Jess, speaking for the both of them.

"There's strawberries and ice-cream to come, if you like?"

Todd and Jess shook their heads. "No thanks."

"Ok, you can go, if you've finished."

Jess and Todd left the table and went upstairs. At first Libby thought they must have homework to do which they'd left until the last minute, but when she went upstairs to run a bath she saw they were talking together in Todd's room. She noticed their voices quieting as she approached the open door on the way to her bedroom. She was curious to know what they were whispering about but thought it best to leave them to it. There was a sense of calm solidarity in the house but it was tinged with an undercurrent of edginess. Any one of them could snap at any moment if someone said the wrong thing.

Later in the evening they watched television together, a couple of light entertainment family shows, but no-one was really paying attention and the audience laughter fell on deaf ears in a silent room. They all went to bed early. Libby didn't feel tired but couldn't concentrate on her book. She was thinking about the last time she'd seen Ella and felt her face redden with shame as she remembered the terrible things she'd been shouting at her. She flicked off the bedside lamp, but the darkness did nothing to dim the images in her head. She heard Todd's light go off in his bedroom next door. He lay there, wide awake too replaying over and over again the scene when Ella had tripped on the rug and fell onto the little wooden table. She had tripped, he was certain of that, he hadn't pushed her, he would never do such a thing but even so he couldn't get it out of his head that it was his fault she had fallen at all.

Jess was crying into her pillow. She had never really had much to do with Ella but she liked her a lot. She was tall and really attractive, a successful writer and a confident woman. Everyone seemed to like her. She had nothing to reproach herself for but she had seen her mother behave badly shouting terrible insults at Ella and she'd seen her own brother's anger too. She loved them both and knew they were feeling bad about what had happened but Jess was also in her own private hell.

Chapter Twenty-Five

Libby and Jess were staring out of the conservatory scanning the panorama for a sight of Todd. A strange hissing noise erupted from the kitchen.

"Jess, go and turn the potatoes down please, quickly. Actually, turn them off, turn everything off and the oven." Jess ran to the kitchen obediently, switched the gas rings off and the oven and ran back to her mother's side.

"I'm going to go and look for him. It's nearly dark already. You're sure he hasn't said anything to you about going somewhere?"

"You've asked me that a hundred times, Mum," said Jess quietly.

"I know I have," snapped Libby. "But you might remember something."

"He didn't say anything. Honestly. We just walked home from sailing club like always. Then he was hanging around with his mates on the beach and I couldn't be bothered waiting for him so I came home."

"Why would he switch his phone off? Why would he do that?"

"Maybe it just ran out of battery."

"Oh god! And what if he needs help and he can't contact me? Right, I'm going out to find him. Fetch me the big torch, in the cupboard by the back door." Again Jess ran to the kitchen, calling back to her mother, "I'm coming with you." She brought the torch back as Libby was putting on her walking shoes.

"No you stay here in case he comes home, and then you can phone me on my mobile."

Ella had spent most of the day mooching around in her dressing gown. She had slept amazingly well the night before but had felt headachey and sluggish all day. By late afternoon she was fed up with herself and her moroseness and had made the effort to have a luxurious bath with her favourite bath cream and body lotion. She felt better for it and was coming to accept that she could actually function perfectly well, despite what had happened to her in the last forty-eight hours.

She tested herself with the thought of food and smiled with sardonic humour at the fact that she never seemed to lose her appetite. Even so, she didn't really feel like cooking and so took a pizza from the freezer, added some extra cheese and herbs to it, switched the oven on and placed the pizza in the middle. As the heat from the oven quickly warmed the kitchen, Ella realised how stuffy it was inside. The house had been shut up now for a few days. She hadn't been out and hadn't even opened a window. She pulled open the back door and took a deep breath of fresh air. It had been a warm sunny day and after the miserable drizzly rain of yesterday there was a smell of earthy dampness in the air which reminded her of a childhood holiday on a farm in Devon.

The evenings were drawing in already. It was only late August but in just one month when the children were back at school the weather would start to turn and autumn would be on the way. Ella sighed, slipping into melancholia. The summer had been too short, she wasn't ready for long dark evenings yet. She stepped out into the garden in her bare feet, the grass cold and tickly between her toes. She looked down to the deserted beach. It would be strewn with a new mass of seaweed and other bits and pieces after the weekend storm. She decided to go down and have a look maybe tomorrow to see if some interesting pieces of driftwood had come ashore that she could use to display in her hut. Ella was just about to return to the kitchen when something on the beach caught her eye. A small light was shining one minute on the sand and the next flicking up into the distance along the beach. She could just about make out the dark figure of someone who was obviously looking for something. Ella continued to stare for some time. There was something familiar about the person on the beach. It was only a dark shape to her from this distance but she could tell it was a woman. And she was quite sure it was Libby.

What was Libby doing down on the beach in the dark? Looking for something, obviously. But what could be so important it couldn't wait until the morning when it was light? Ella continued to watch for a few seconds more. Suddenly, the spotlight moved frantically from one direction to the other, finally circling three hundred and sixty degrees in hopeless desperation. Ella couldn't make sense of it at all. She peered into the darkness, squinting hard to identify some feature which would confirm to her it was definitely Libby down there all alone on the beach.

She would phone. Where was her mobile? It felt like ages since Ella had had to deal with everyday normalities like using a phone. For a second she couldn't even think where to look for her mobile. She had to retrace her steps over the last couple of days before she could backtrack to where it might be. It was on her bedside table, she always took it up to bed with her as there wasn't a phone upstairs. It was still there from when she'd taken it up after the charity party. She hadn't even thought to take it with her to the hospital; it had been a morning of such fear and panic.

She grabbed it now and searched for Libby's name, tapping the call button immediately. She ran back down the stairs and out to the garden, scanning the beach for the familiar figure but struggling with the darkness now her eyes were accustomed to the indoor artificial light. She could see Libby and squinted again to detect movement which would indicate she was answering her phone but the figure did not move.

"Hello. Todd? Is that you?"

"Hello. No. It's Ella. Who's that?"

Ella had meant to call Libby's mobile phone but in her haste, she must have phoned Libby's home number by mistake.

"It's Jess."

"Hello Jess. I was after your mum. Is she there? Or?"

"No, she's not here. She's out; she's looking for Todd. He hasn't come home tonight. And I don't know where he is. He didn't say anything to me. Honestly, I don't know where he could be." There was silence and then Ella could hear the young girl crying; short, muffled sobs which she was trying hard to control.

"Jess, is your mum on the beach? I think I can see her looking around."

"Yes, I think so."

"Ok, now listen. I'm going down to join her. I'll help her find him. Now, don't worry, put the phone down in case Todd calls and hopefully we'll all be back soon." Ella heard the phone click off. She dashed back upstairs to change into her jeans and a t-shirt. She ran down the steps to the beach, through the dark, quickly catching up with Libby, calling out to her just a short distance away. Libby jumped and turned to face Ella, clutching her chest.

"Oh my god! Oh, Ella, it's you." Libby didn't know what to say. A few hours ago she was still trying to summon the courage to go and apologise to Ella. She had wanted to go and chat with her friend and ask if there was anything she could do to help. But here, at this moment her mind was going wild with fearful thoughts for her son. She couldn't handle Ella and her tragedy at this time and thankfully, she didn't have to. As if Ella knew what was going through Libby's head, she simply asked, "Can I help you look for Todd?"

"Do you know something? Do you know where he is?"

"No, I'm afraid I don't but just let me help will you?" All sorts of thoughts were spinning in Ella's mind. Was Todd in some kind of trouble? He was really angry about her donating that money to charity. Maybe he needed it to pay someone off for something. What had she done? Had she put him in danger? The kiss on her birthday then discovering she was pregnant by his grandfather. Was it all too much for a seventeen year old? Somehow she felt responsible.

"I thought he might have come down to the beach. He likes to fish over by those rocks."

"I don't think he's stayed out tonight to go fishing Libby."

"No, I suppose not," said Libby quietly, feeling stupid at her silly comment and realising how all over the place she was, and how relieved she was that Ella was taking control.

"Come on, let's go to the far end. I wonder if he's hiding out at the huts." Ella had brought her own torch with her and led the way, shining the light in and amongst the huts, in between their wooden steps and mini terraces. It didn't look as if he was there and then just as they were getting level with Ella's hut, they heard a scuffle and a voice called out in the darkness.

"Mum?" They shone their torches in the direction of the voice to see Todd scramble to his feet from where he'd been huddled in the corner on the deck of Ella's hut.

"Todd, is that you? Thank god."

Todd was blinded by the double spot light but as they approached he was able to make out the second person.

"Oh no Mum, not Ella." His voice cracked as if he'd been crying. "It's my fault. It's all my fault." He sat on the steps and sank his head in his hands. Libby was sitting at his side in an instant putting her arm around him but Ella stayed a little way back.

"It's all my fault. All because of the money. I made her fall. And now her baby's dead because of me."

Now Ella rushed forward and kneeled in the sand at Todd's feet.

"No Todd, it wasn't your fault. It was no-one's fault, just one of those things."

Todd lifted his face to see his mother look from him to Ella back to him again, completely confused. Ella was silent and Todd, even though he was exhausted, tired and hungry, knew this was his job to explain. "Mum, I need to talk to you."

"Alright, well let's get home shall we?"

They made their way back up the beach, Libby with her arm around her son all the way home, not willing to let go of him, relief flooding through her. As they arrived level with Ella's cottage, she made to go inside and leave them to it but Todd didn't want that.

"No, you come too Ella. I want her to come with us Mum."

"Well, of course she can if she wants to."

Jess was at the conservatory window keeping watch. She dashed to the back door as they bustled inside, delighted to see her brother alive and well but a bit cross too. "Mum, you should've phoned me to say you'd found him," she whispered.

"Sorry darling, I didn't think, we just came straight home. Anyway, it's alright now." She gave her daughter a special smile, grateful her family were all safe and at home. Libby led the way through to the lounge. Jess sat next to Todd and Ella sat on the settee opposite.

"Right, first things first, I'll put the kettle on. Todd, do you want tea or cocoa?"

"Tea please. In my big mug." Libby turned to return to the kitchen.

"Can I have cocoa?" called out an affronted Jess, a little miffed that her brother was getting all the special attention, and for what? For not coming home and making everyone worry about him! And now Todd called out, "Is there anything to eat? I'm starving."

Suddenly Ella jumped up. "Oh crikey! I have a pizza in the oven. It'll be burnt to a crisp." She looked at her watch and was surprised to see they hadn't been out as long as she thought.

"Actually, it might be ok. I'll pop back and get it." Ella returned a couple of minutes later with the pizza on a plate, already sliced and covered in foil. "It's not a family sized one or anything but there's enough to share."

Libby had already brought in the tea things and now handed out plates to everyone as they each devoured a slice of hot cheesy pizza.

A couple of hours later, Todd and Jess were in bed and Libby and Ella were sharing a bottle of wine. Todd had confessed to his mother about the money-making scam he'd been involved in. He also admitted to breaking in to Ella's hut and using it as a hiding place. He wondered if Jess would make her own confession that she used the hut too hoping it might lessen his crime but his sister was unusually cowardly quiet this evening. He provided an edited version of events at Francine's party, avoiding eye contact with Ella and hoping she wouldn't fill in the missing bits – relieved that she didn't. Ella reassured him again that the fall was an accident and had done nothing to contribute to her losing her baby. She spoke to them both as she explained the few medical details she'd been given and confirmed nothing whatsoever could have prevented what was in effect nature's way, as cruel and unfair as it seemed sometimes.

"I'm sorry Libby, for not finding a way to tell you about Todd and the money and everything. I didn't want to make trouble. I'd only been here five minutes, but I realise now I should have told you."

"Mm, yes," agreed Libby smiling kindly, "but I do understand, you were in an awkward spot there for a while."

"Even so, I had no right to keep it from you."

"I owe you an apology too. I had no right saying what I did at the party. I'm so ashamed of myself." Libby's face was colouring red as she recalled her behaviour that night.

"Oh come on, we could go on like this all night. Let's just forget it and put it all behind us."

"Agreed. Let's finish this bottle." Libby poured the last of the wine between their glasses. She was thinking about Andrew but didn't have the energy or the inclination to ask anything. She was more than happy that she and Ella had resumed their friendship. Ella was thinking about him too and was grateful Libby hadn't asked anything. She wasn't clear in her own mind how things stood between her and Andrew, let alone explain to someone else. She finished her wine and tried unsuccessfully to stifle a yawn. She was suddenly so tired she could have curled up there and then on Libby's settee and fallen asleep.

They plodded in silence through the kitchen to the back door, quiet and tired. The drama and subsequent relief of the evening finally draining them of energy.

"Thanks for coming down to the beach to help. It was really kind of you, after, well you know, after everything."

"It's ok, anyway, that's what friends are for."

"I know. And you are a very good friend to me."

"Yes I am. Not like the likes of Francine Lawrence!"

"Oh my god! That woman! How can I ever face her again?"

"Would you want to? Anyway, I'm going home to my bed, we can talk about this another time – if you'd like to."

"Yes I would like to, thanks." Libby reached up and gave Ella a big hug and Ella felt overwhelming comfort from the genuine gesture of affection. She simply allowed herself to be hugged for a few seconds. Both women were a little tearful and only Libby was able to speak. "Take care, I'll see you tomorrow."

Chapter Twenty-Six

Ella had woken early. It was too warm to laze in bed and besides she didn't want to give her mind full of thoughts time or space to kick into action. She showered and dressed and was sitting in front of her laptop at the kitchen table before eight o'clock. It was a good idea to immerse herself in work even if she was only surfing the internet looking for inspiration for future articles. She needed to consider winter topics as the monthly magazines usually worked six months ahead but on such a gorgeous August day, she found it almost impossible to even think about frost and snow. And the new year ahead seemed a million miles away, just as the winter at the beginning of this year seemed a lifetime ago.

Ella just couldn't get her head around focusing on winter. The first thing that came to mind was Christmas and families and delivering of presents. If things had been different she would have had the most special Christmas delivery ever and would never want for another present again. But she didn't want to think about that. She gave up on searching for a writing idea and simply allowed herself to wander through the internet stumbling onto a website selling cake decorating supplies and from there to a site selling very expensive hand knitted sweaters which of course had a section for babies and toddlers wear. Ella managed to resist clicking on the link and closed the laptop down, scraping back her chair noisily as she got up to get a cold drink.

She heard a car door slam and looked up to see Andrew's car parked on the lane outside Libby's house. She hadn't seen him since the party and really hoped he wouldn't call on her now. She still didn't feel she could face him and the inevitable discussion they should have about their relationship.

Ella darted backwards as she saw Andrew at the end of her drive, coming towards the cottage. In a split second, she considered running upstairs and pretending to be out or asleep but she wasn't sure Andrew hadn't caught a glimpse of her at the window. And anyway it was too late now, he was in the back garden and they were in full view of each other. There was no way out, they would have to talk.

Ella held the door open as he stepped inside, taking a couple of seconds to wipe his feet on the mat even though there was really no need to. As he looked up, Ella instinctively turned away and grabbed the kettle.

"Tea?"

"Yes please, lovely."

The kettle filled, Ella leaned against the sink, facing Andrew squarely, trying to remember the easy smile she always used to have for him. He stepped forward and kissed her gently on her cheek. There were no enveloping hugs, no passionate kisses, just an unspoken understanding between them that there probably wouldn't be any of those any more.

"So, how are you?"

"Fine. Physically anyway. Apparently." Ella's smile faded.

Andrew nodded, not really wanting to get into the mechanics of the aftercare of a woman who's had a miscarriage. When his children were born, he wasn't even allowed into the delivery room.

"Thank you for helping Libby, look for Todd and everything."

"It's ok, I was glad to help."

A few seconds of silence passed. Andrew glanced at the clock on the wall and Ella jumped as the electric kettle switched itself off. She busied herself with making tea while Andrew pulled out a chair and sat down at the table. Ella sneaked a sideways glance at him as she poured milk into the mugs. He looked weary today, older than his sixty-three years. This was all too much for him Ella realised, a little sadly. Nothing, but nothing in the world would ever make her say that things had turned out for the best but she thought this must be what Andrew was thinking. And she knew, too, that this kind man would be struggling with his thoughts, knowing as he did how much she wanted this baby.

Ella placed the mugs on the table, caught Andrew's eye and held his gaze, hoping her smile conveyed some of the understanding she felt even though she had no way of putting it into words. It occurred to her she would find it easier to write all this down than speak about it, and she liked the logic of this. After all, she was a writer. Andrew sipped his tea, and again Ella looked across at him, trying to gauge her feelings. He was a very attractive man, solid and sure of himself and his desires. The word 'fatherly' came to Ella's mind and she felt her cheeks redden at whatever that might mean. Andrew was easily old enough to be her father and them some. She hoped he wouldn't look up and see her blushing. Had that been all she was looking for, a father figure? Someone to look after her? No, it had been much more than that. There had been a real passion, an excitement at being attracted to and attractive to a man after all the years with Jon.

Ella leant back in her chair. Was there a chance she and Andrew would pick up together again? Did she want that? She had to decide. It was only fair to herself and Andrew to make a decision.

"I'm going away for a while Ella."

"Oh, where are you off to?"

"Italy. For a painting course, holiday type of thing. I booked it a few weeks ago with some friends."

"It sounds great. You'll have a lovely time painting everyday. When do you leave?"

"At the weekend."

Ella felt immediate relief that Andrew would be away for a while and from that she had to acknowledge a certain question had been answered. She was genuinely pleased for him that he was going to Italy to do something he loved but her overwhelming feeling was a sense of freedom that they wouldn't be running into each other over the next few weeks. It was interesting, she thought, to think he had only booked it a few weeks ago which proved he had no intention of taking her with him.

She wasn't ready to say things had worked out for the best but the words were beginning to gather together somewhere in the depths of her mind. Maybe she would see the picture clearer one day.

Andrew didn't stay long enough to finish his tea. He made some attempt at a joke about starting his packing. Ella rinsed the mugs in the sink, confident that once Andrew had been on holiday and returned from Italy, they would both have moved on a little further.

Chapter Twenty-Seven

Ella lifted the calendar from the kitchen wall and flipped the page over. The picture showed a display of squashes and pumpkins in a range of autumnal colours from pale gold through to sunset orange. It was the first of October. Ella looked at the empty calendar page as she hung it back on its hook. Her eyes were immediately drawn to the thirtieth of the month. It would be on a Sunday this year, last year a Saturday of course, the day Jon got married.

Ella looked at the mass of paperwork sprawled over the kitchen table. She had been working full throttle, doing well with a difficult three thousand word article until she'd been disturbed by a phone call. And now she was fiddling about with mindless tasks like refilling the sugar bowl and watering plants. She knew it would be impossible to resume her writing, she wouldn't be able to concentrate. She reckoned she'd have Jon on her mind for the rest of the day now.

Ella decided to pop next door to see Libby. She hadn't seen her for a couple of days and she fancied a chat. Libby was bound to be planning a Halloween party or maybe something for Bonfire Night and it would be a good distraction to see if she could help out in any way.

Unusually, Libby was sitting down in the kitchen with a mug of coffee when Ella arrived, tapping on the back door and letting herself in, making Libby jump.

"Oops, sorry, you looked miles away there."

Libby immediately stood up as if she'd been caught out doing something she shouldn't.

"Yes, well, I was wishing I was miles away anyway. Preferably somewhere hot and sunny and exotic. Libby sighed and glanced up at her pin board full of neatly arranged notices and reminders. Ella followed her gaze and saw a post-card from Italy showing an enticing view of the Adriatic Cost of Puglia in the south of the country. She hadn't received a post-card from Andrew and hadn't seen him since he'd been back. Neither Libby nor Ella mentioned the post-card.

"Are you ok? I just popped over for a quick chat but if it's not a good time?"

"No, don't be silly. It's always lovely to see you. I was just a bit thoughtful that's all."

"Anything I can help with?"

"No, not really. I'm just a little fed up that's all. Shall we have hot chocolate?"

Ella nodded as Libby put full fat creamy milk in the microwave and spooned good quality cocoa powder into mugs.

"It's not like you Libby to be fed up. What's wrong?"

"Everything! Everything's going wrong." Libby smiled and tried to laugh at herself but didn't quite manage it.

"Oh come on, it can't be that bad."

Ella looked around at Libby's immaculate kitchen, everything tidy and in its place as always. It seemed to Ella that Libby had a pretty good life.

"Think about all the things going right. You have two lovely children."

Libby raised her eyebrows.

"Yes you do. And you have Andrew and this gorgeous house."

"Well, I might not have it much longer." Libby poured the hot milk into the mugs and stirred so vigorously, it slopped onto the worktop. She grabbed a cloth and wiped it clean then placed the mugs on the small low table between the armchairs at the side of the kitchen. They had just sat down when Libby jumped up again and brought a bag of mini marshmallows from the cupboard.

"You can't have hot chocolate without marshmallows," she said as she shook a few from the bag into her mug before handing the bag to Ella. Her forced cheeriness was evident as was her brave smile.

"What do you mean Libby? About the house?"

Libby took her mug in both hands, closed her eyes and sipped the hot chocolate. "My ex-husband, David, he's leaving his very good job at the university and going on a year's teaching sabbatical in Ghana."

"Oh, is it something he's always wanted to do?"

"He mentioned it a few months ago. I didn't pay that much attention, I didn't think he was serious. He must be having a mid-life crisis or something."

"Wow! A big decision for him, and for Todd and Jess too.

"He's told them they can go out and visit but I don't know who's going to pay. He's already informed me my income will be dramatically reduced. I don't really know what it all means. Will I have to sell the house? Will he still provide for the children? They're over sixteen, he's not obliged to."

"Crikey, Libby, you've got a lot to talk about."

"Mm, deep discussions, about finances of all things, with ex-husbands, is not top of my favourite things to do list."

Now it was Ella's turn to be deep in thought. She was thinking about Jon, his forth-coming first wedding anniversary on which he would be alone.

"Ella? Have I said something?"

"No, of course not. I was just thinking about my own ex-husband, that's all."

"Yes, my god, he's certainly been through it, hasn't he, over the last few months?"

Ella finished her hot chocolate, nodding as she placed the mug on the table.

"And now I'm being completely insensitive Ella. You've had enough to deal with too. And here I am whingeing because my ex-husband has actually got a life and is getting on with it."

Ella didn't really know what to say without it sounding banal. She knew Libby didn't have to go out to work but she didn't really know how she filled her days. Libby took the mugs and rinsed them in the sink, swishing away the thick chocolaty dregs.

"Listen Ella, have you got anything you need to rush back home for?"

"No, not really, some work but it can wait."

"It's Saturday, you shouldn't have to work on a Saturday. Right, let's get out of here before we end up slitting our wrists. Fancy a walk along the beach?"

"Sounds perfect, just what we need."

They strolled along, side by side, in easy silence. The sky had clouded over and despite being outdoors in the fresh air, the dreary grey clouds reflected their mood. The beach was surprisingly empty for a Saturday afternoon although it did seem to be getting darker by the second. Libby thought she felt spots of rain and held out her hands, palms up. She and Ella looked at each other with matching expressions that said 'typical, just our luck'.

"What shall we do? Go back to mine or run for it somewhere else?"

"Shall we go to the hut?"

"Great idea."

It was only a light drizzle but they quickened their pace and by the time they got to the beach hut the rain was coming down heavier. Ella unlocked and went inside while Libby leant against the wooden railing on the terrace looking out along the beach. An elderly couple out walking their dog were hurrying away as quick as they could which wasn't very quick at all on the soft sand. Just behind them were two young boys, ambling along, not minding one bit that they were getting soaking wet.

"Do you want a hot drink?" asked Ella, "or I have a bottle of red." Libby grinned. "Red it is then." She appeared a minute later, and handed Libby a generously filled glass of wine.

"I like the rain," said Ella.

"Mm, so do I. If I'm not out in it."

"Yeah, not so good if you're out in it and on your bike."

"Not so good if you're out in it, and on your bike and in a bikini."

"When have you ever been out in the rain on your bike in a bikini?"

Libby raised her eyebrows and grinned. "Too much information Libby!" They giggled and then fell quiet, standing side by side, looking at the rain which was hammering down now. The rainwater merged silently with the sea but it fell noisily onto the wet sand. Ella took a deep breath. "Did you know around seventy-five per cent of the earth's surface is covered in water?"

"Mm, is it?"

Ella stared out over the sea to the horizon. It was fascinating just to stand and stare at the huge expanse of water, comforting and yet slightly frightening at the same time. She was thinking how the whole world was separated by and yet connected by seas and oceans and that it was no wonder people shared a fascination of them. "This is nice, it's not too cold either. Are you ok out here?"

"Yes, it's lovely."

Libby took Ella's glass of wine while Ella dragged two comfy wicker chairs onto the terrace. They settled themselves and sat in silence for a while sipping their wine and staring out to sea. The rain had eased just a little but it was constant; the straight down determined type of rain which would probably last all afternoon.

"When is David off to Ghana?"

"I'm not exactly sure. Soon I think."

"It doesn't give you long to sort things out."

"Exactly, he could have given me more notice."

"Perhaps that's a good thing. Maybe he doesn't expect you to sell the house."

Libby shrugged. "I don't know. He won't be earning. What else can I do?"

"It's only for a year. Perhaps he's made provisions. And also maybe, you know, you could go back to work yourself?"

"As an air hostess? I'd love to but I'm a bit long in the tooth for that! And a job in a super-market isn't going to pay my mortgage."

Ella felt as if she was treading on sensitive ground and thought it best to let the moment go.

"I'm sorry Ella. I know how it must look. I've been very fortunate in how David has provided for us. It's meant I haven't had to go out to work. And David wanted that too, he likes the idea of me being here for the children if they need me. But yes, I've been spoilt. And it's quite right he should do his thing. I would go out to work but what can I do after all these years?"

"There are loads of things you could do. You could get into event organising for one thing, it's a big industry these days. You did a brilliant job with Francine's party."

"Apart from the bit where I got piddled and made a pass at the hostess's husband."

"Ok, so don't put that bit on your CV. But the rest of it was fantastic."

"Mm, I don't know. It's one thing to organise something locally for people you know and when it's for charity people can be very forgiving. But for real and for money, I don't know, it's a big responsibility."

"Yes, but something to think about. And you could start small. Organise hen parties, baby showers, things like that, in people's homes. You could do the whole lot, decorations, catering and even the hand-written invitations. Libby, there are loads of things you have a talent for. You could teach calligraphy for one thing. From your own gorgeous home, lay on lunch, hours to suit yourself, your own business – it could be perfect."

Ella had Libby's attention. She was captivated, her face animated.

"My god, Ella! I'd never thought of doing any of those things. I would just love to teach calligraphy. Imagine that, having my own business."

Yep, and if you don't fancy people traipsing around your home, you could buy that burnt out beach hut there. It's going for a snip. Do it up and hold calligraphy courses from there. It would add an extra dimension of quirkiness."

"How do you know it's for sale? I've been after one of these huts for years."

"Ah-ha! It seems I'm a local here now and I get included in the local gossip."

"Hmm." Libby was a little put out that she hadn't heard about the hut being for sale but her mind was too busy for it to last. "Well, let's drink to all that. To good ideas." They chinked their glasses.

"To good ideas," repeated Ella.

Libby spotted someone further up the beach, a jogger jogging at a steady pace and coming towards them.

"Oh dear, I bet he wished he'd brought his pak-a-mac," said Libby, smiling and feeling much happier than she had for ages. As the jogger got nearer, they both recognised him as Neil Cookson. Libby held up her glass. "Afternoon doctor."

Neil stopped in front of the hut smiling up at them. "Afternoon ladies, I hope you're not exceeding your recommended daily units?"

"Certainly not," said Libby comically slurring.

"Would you like a drink?" said Ella, conscious of and a little embarrassed at the nearly empty wine bottle beside their feet. Neil Cookson jogged up the steps.

"I'd love a glass of water please." Ella disappeared into the hut and brought out a small bottle of mineral water while Libby took a sneaky sideways glance, up and down, at the very nice-looking doctor. And was it her imagination or was Ella a little tongue-tied? Neil finished his drink and handed the bottle back to Ella. "Thanks."

"Would you like to shelter here for a while, you know, until it stops raining?"

"No, it's ok thanks. I'm wet through already, can't get any wetter. I'm off home for a hot shower."

"Mm-mm," came suggestively from Libby as Ella silently mouthed to Neil that she'd obviously had too much wine.

"See you around," said Neil, smiling. "Bye Libby, take it easy," he called out as he jogged down the steps and away down the beach giving a wave as he passed. Ella sat down and waited for the inevitable comment Libby would be unable to resist making. It only took a second.

"Nice, isn't he?" she said, staring straight ahead.

"Mm, he is," said Ella non-committal.

"Fit. Isn't that what they say now?"

Ella laughed. "Libby!"

"I'm just saying. I've never seen him with so few clothes on and he looks fit. He looks after himself, that's all I mean, and so he should, he's a doctor."

"You're terrible. This is the last time I give you wine in the middle of the day."

"Don't worry, I'm fine. I'm just teasing."

"Ok, we might as well finish this last bit." Ella shared the last of the wine between them.

"Talking of doctors and things, have you heard from Colette recently? How's her father?"

"Actually, I spoke to him this morning, he phoned me."

"Really? What did he want?"

"He wants to come and see me."

"Does he? What for?"

"I don't know. He wouldn't say."

"Well, that's a bit rude. He wants to come and see you after all this time but he won't say why. He's got a bit of a nerve."

"No, it wasn't like that. I think he was on a mobile and it wasn't a good line. It was like he didn't really want to chat, he just wanted me to agree to meet him. He seemed relieved when I said yes and that was it."

"What do you think he wants?"

"I don't know. I have no idea."

"Do you think he's going to ask you back?"

"I've been wondering about it. I can't imagine he would. But then again, I never imagined he would ever leave me either. A year ago, I would've gone back with him like a shot. But the truth is, I haven't thought like that for ages now. I can't even remember when I stopped thinking about him in that way. I've no idea how I feel."

"When are you meeting him?"

"Next Saturday at three o'clock."

"Where?"

"Here, at the hut."

Chapter Twenty-Eight

Ella spent considerable time deciding what to wear. Should she make a special effort? Or should she make no effort at all? Either way, she would be making a statement which in itself was confusing as she still didn't know why Jon wanted to see her. They hadn't spoken since last week. She finally came to the conclusion she didn't want to make any kind of statement and that it really didn't matter what she wore. Jon obviously had something to say and it wasn't going to be dependent on her outfit. She pulled on her smartest jeans and a thick polo neck sweater. It was a mild day and she decided to do without a jacket.

Ella left the cottage a few minutes before three o'clock and walked towards her beach hut. It wasn't long before she could see someone was already there, sitting halfway up the steps. She couldn't see clearly but could just about make out the familiar figure of her ex-husband. She quickened her pace a little and could feel her heart pounding faster as she got nearer. What on earth was he going to say to her? Just a few minutes more and she would know what this was all about.

As she got a little closer, Ella could see Jon had his knees drawn up close to his body and was holding something on his lap, and there were various bags on the steps by his feet. Had he bought her presents, she wondered, was that what he thought it would take to get her back?

Ella stood at the bottom of the steps looking up at Jon. She hadn't seen him for almost a year and then it had been from behind a tree on his wedding day. He had looked well that day, even at a distance from her hiding place. He'd looked healthy and happy. But now, she hardly recognised the man in front of her. He was thin, bony and his skin was colourless, almost grey. The shock was like a rock to her head. She'd almost forgotten he'd been seriously ill or was it that she'd chosen to put it out of her mind. There was definitely no denying it now, Jon looked like a frail old man and she wasn't sure if he would be able to stand up unaided.

"Hello Ella, how are you?"

"Hello. I'm ok." It seemed crass to return the normally courteous question and Ella looked away from Jon's face and at the bundle he was holding carefully in his lap. It was a baby. His daughter. Her stomach lurched. And for a second she felt like turning right around and going back home and leaving him there. What was he thinking? Did he expect her to coo and fuss over his baby? Tell him she had his nose or his sticky out ears or whatever? How bloody insensitive of him to bring her along. Jon could see the anxiety on her face.

"Thanks for coming. You're probably wondering why I asked to see you."

Jon's voice was weak and Ella could just about hear him. Reluctantly she moved forward a little.

"Yes, I am." She looked back along the beach, as if she had something she was impatient to get back to. This was difficult, seeing Jon like this and with his baby too. She realised, feeling rather stupid, she assumed this meeting would be less unpleasant than this.

"I have the biggest favour to ask of you. In fact, the word favour doesn't even come close. And it would be something I can never repay you for. Quite literally." Jon smiled feebly. Ella frowned. She couldn't guess what Jon was talking about. Time seemed to stand still; every second felt like forever and Ella thought she would scream if she didn't know soon what Jon was going on about. What could he possibly want her to do? She stood there waiting, too scared to ask.

Jon stood up, slowly and carefully, and descended the wooden steps, standing close beside Ella on the sand.

"This is Isobel."

Ella had no choice but to look at the baby, bundled in blankets, nestling in Jon's arms. She was gorgeous, fast asleep, her long lashes motionless against her perfect baby skin. Ella looked up into Jon's face. Up close, she was even more shocked to see how ravaged he looked. His lined skin was translucent and his watery eyes looked hopeless. Ella's eyes were beginning to water too. She struggled to speak. "She's beautiful."

"Yes, but without a mother and not much of a father either."

"I'm sure you're doing your best."

"It's not good enough. I can't manage. Not on my own."

"No, I suppose it can't be easy. Colette must be a god-send for you at the moment."

"She is but it's not fair to put all this on her. This was her idea actually. I needed some persuading but she managed to convince me. She brought me down, she's waiting for me." Jon nodded his head in the direction of the road, behind the huts, above the beach. Ella looked up and saw Colette sitting in the driver's seat of Jon's car. She waved and smiled tentatively. Ella smiled back.

"I'd like you to look after Isobel." There he'd said it. Ella was surprised by her calmness. It was as if, in the eternity of the last few seconds, she knew this was coming.

"Oh Jon, I don't know." With the back of her little finger, she stroked Isobel's smooth cheek. The bond was made. There was no going back. She wanted to hold her and instinctively Jon passed Isobel over and laid her in Ella's arms. Ella smiled, surprised at the weight of this little being. "I suppose I could help out for a while." Ella couldn't take her eyes off Isobel. "My god, it'll be difficult giving her back though. Unless she screams my house down, and then I suppose I might be glad to give her back." Ella laughed but the laughter soon stopped when she looked up at Jon's sad face. He closed his eyes and shook his head as a tear squeezed from each eye and slid down his face.

"Jon? This is just until you get better, isn't it? How long, do you think?"

Jon kept his eyes closed and shook his head again, temporarily unable to speak.

"Jon?" Ella's eyes were filled with tears too. She knew now, with certainty, what was to come. She knew her ex-husband, they could still communicate without speaking.

Finally Jon opened his eyes. "There is no getting better, Ella." Ella knew it, but still she gasped at the horror of it all. Jon stroked his daughter's head. "I don't have much time, Ella."

"You have to go? Now?" Ella looked up at Colette in the car. She wanted them all to come back home with her and maybe all together, safely, they could sort this out.

"Yes, I do have to go, I think it's best. But that's not what I meant. What I'm saying is, I probably won't be here to see this little one's first birthday, I'm afraid." The tears were streaming down Ella's face and she made no attempt to stop them.

"You can visit, whenever you want," she managed to say.

"Probably not. I think it's all down hill pretty quickly from here on. You understand why I'm doing this Ella? I know this is what you've always wanted and I'm so sorry it's happened like this. I'm so sorry. Please say you're happy to do this. Not for me, I'm not asking for me. But for Isobel, there's no-one I'd rather ask to be her mother."

Ella nodded, unable to speak. She managed to utter two words while nodding frantically in an effort to convince him. "Happy. Yes."

Jon put his arm around Ella's shoulders and rested his head against hers. He kissed the top of her head, then leant forward and kissed his baby's forehead, turning finally to smile at Ella before walking away. Ella reached out to grab his hand but missed. She watched him walk slowly and painfully round the hut, up the beach and back onto the road. It seemed to take him forever and considerable effort to get into the car.

Ella locked eyes with Colette as they drove away. Colette nodded and smiled and Ella knew she would be seeing her very soon and probably a lot more of her too which was a comforting thought. They would need and help each other for a long time to come.

"Mum, what have I told you about being a nosey neighbour?"

"Oh shush Jess, I'm just looking."

Jess winced. Her mother was unusually on edge this afternoon. She joined her over at the window.

"What's up? What are you looking for?"

"It's Ella. She's meeting with her ex-husband today, on the beach."

"How romantic."

"No, I don't think it's a romantic thing. It might be. I just hope she's ok."

"Do you ever think about getting back with Dad?"

Libby was momentarily taken aback by the directness of the question, but of course it was normal her daughter would think about it.

"No love. It's right we're not together anymore."

"Are you glad he's only going to Ghana for six months though? Means we get to stay in the house doesn't it?"

"Well, yes, it does. But actually I've got some ideas of my own so I don't have to rely on your dad so much financially in future."

"Oh right. Look, is that Ella on the beach? She's not with anyone."

Libby squinted through the window. "Yes, it is her, isn't it? She's heading home. They weren't together long then. What's she's carrying? Loads of bags and things? Perhaps I should give her a call, make sure she's alright."

Jess gave her a look. "You're a good friend to her Mum, but she knows where you are, if she needs you."

"Yes, you're right. She knows where I am. I'll leave her to it today."

Jess's look changed to one of approval and Libby felt better for it, if not a little amused to be given advice from her teenage daughter.

Ella was still cuddling baby Isobel late into the night. She couldn't bear to put her down. Her thoughts and feelings were vacillating between wonder and jubilation at having this beautiful baby, right here and now, to bring up as her own daughter and intense sadness at the tragic circumstances that allowed it to happen.

A gentle but firm knock on the door made Ella jump and the baby fidgeted and whimpered at being disturbed. Ella instinctively held her tighter as if the person at the door had come to take her away. She held her breath and stayed where she was on the armchair in her favourite place in the kitchen. Whoever it was knocked again, a little louder this time. Ella placed Isobel in her basket on the kitchen table and tucked the blankets snugly around her. She'd turned the decrepit heating up to full blast and realised for the first time how warm it was. She walked slowly to the front door, still hoping whoever it was had given up and gone away. But she could see someone through the stained glass window although she couldn't make out who it was.

Ella opened the door just a little, wary now of whoever was calling so late. It took a second or two to make out the face in the dark, a familiar friendly face with a very concerned look on it.

"Hi Ella, it's only me, are you alright?"

"Oh god, thank goodness it's you. Come in." Ella opened the door and stood back, exhausted but relieved to see Neil Cookson standing smiling in her hallway.

"Are you ok? You looked terrified just then."

"I'm fine but yes I was terrified, wondering who was at my door this late at night."

"Sorry, I was on my way home and your house looked odd, with all its curtains open and only one little light on. I was, well, a little worried about you."

"Were you? Oh, thank-you. This was too much for Ella to take in, all in one day. "Do you want to come through for a drink?"

"If you're sure. And why are you up so late? It's nearly two o'clock in the morning."

"Come in, I'll show you." Ella was behaving very odd thought Neil. She had a calm sereneness about her and a mysterious smile which was baffling him. He followed her into the kitchen and saw the basket on the table with Ella standing over it, her face flushed pink with happiness and a smile that lit her face. But Neil was worried.

"Ella? Where did this baby come from?"

Ella laughed at the prospect of having to explain to the local doctor about the birds and the bees. But she realised the joke wasn't appropriate seeing the look on Neil's face; he looked genuinely concerned for her.

"It's ok, I haven't done anything wrong. Her name is Isobel. Isobel Peters. She's Jon's daughter.

A glimmer of understanding was spreading over Neil's face as he relaxed.

"Sit down Neil, let me explain."

Ella made hot chocolate while Neil sat in her favourite armchair. She handed him a mug and perched on the arm of the chair. "I think this is, in a surreal way, one of the happiest days of my life." They chinked mugs.

"In that case, I've very happy to be sharing it with you," said Neil smiling up at her.

"Me too, very happy."